the planner and the prince

prince

A Spare Change Story

maude winters

For my dear friends who refuse to keep to spa voices.

foreword

This book is a love letter to all the towns on the southwest Michigan shoreline. While it is largely inspired by my childhood time spent in New Buffalo, it could be set in many lovely small towns within the region I call home.

I grew up in La Porte, Indiana just about fifteen minutes from the fictional Buffalo Shores. Some of my fondest memories growing up took root at the Dunes National Park (then the National Lakeshore), Warren Dunes State Park, and New Buffalo's public beach. Now, living back here in Michigan with my family, my daughter is making the same wonderful memories.

This region is a perfect setting for a wedding. Many of the people who arrive in the area spend their summer in cute lakeside cottages. While Patrick and George do not live like normies, they do live like some of the Chicago elites who own massive second homes on the shoreline. Many of the scenes are inspired by actual venues in the area where moments might take place. I imagined Patrick and George's wedding as markedly different from the state occasions and royal weddings I've written to-date. It's beachy, it's casual, and it's just one big party. There is no shortage of love between these two.

The spa scene in the book was inspired by an actual

encounter I had with friends while at a spa in New Buffalo. We were told to keep spa voices. It made us all laugh heartily and just added to my desire to write that scene in. Paul is exuberant and I wanted that to show.

As for Paul's neurodivergence, it is an important part of who he is. Yes, he is exuberant and has a love of life. However, he's often misunderstood. He is a sweetheart. And while some see his neurodivergence as a challenge, Sanne just sees it as another part of his backstory. She can relate in a way. And, in my own neurodivergence, I relate. Paul is dear to me. I've been writing him since he was a toddler and I have always seem him as being real like this. If you are neurodivergent, just know that I get it. It's a part of Paul's life that makes him different. It also makes him a lovely uncle, a great brother, and a wonderful partner for someone who cannot see the forest for the trees.

If you are inspired by this book to travel to the "real" Buffalo Shores, I recommend New Buffalo Beach, Weko Beach (just north in Bridgman), or Warren Dunes State Park. If you want to visit New Buffalo proper (which I recommend you do), visit Oinks for ice cream and Redamak's for a good burger. Get there early and note they don't take card. Get an Oberon for me!

princely problems

. . .

sanne

I rolled out of bed, cursing Darren's alarm. It never woke him. Just me. If I stayed in bed, mine would go off in approximately three minutes. I would hit snooze three or four times and miss my crucial first appointment. Darren was passed out, no response. I swore under my breath, turned off his alarm, and stood over him, concerned about how deeply he always slept. The man didn't drink. How could he sleep so well?

"Darren! Up!" I used a firm but not-too-shrill voice.

It was hard not to hate him. I knew that while he claimed to have a busy day, he started at 8:30 with a HIIT workout, then a 45-minute shower, and arrived at work around 10. His trainer was a relentless man, Hans, who might have passed as Arnold Schwarzenegger. Darren managed a hedge fund. He always wanted to measure up to the amount of time I spent working with clients. I was, for better or worse, available round-the-clock. I am part-therapist, part fixer. He managed other rich people's money.

We both dealt with the rich and powerful too much, but under different guises. While he occasionally talked investors off a ledge, that was the first—and most important—line in my job description. Sometimes, I wondered if I was good for Darren or if my drama only stressed him out. It wasn't really *my* drama, after all. It was the drama my clients brought into my life. And, while I could say I hated it, I lived for it. It was so fulfilling to fix the big, expensive problems of others. It was even better when they thanked me with a nice, fat bonus or gift.

Darren looked up. "I hate mornings."

Boy, don't I know!

I murmured, "I am getting into the shower."

Darren set a second alarm and rolled over. Oh, well, I tried. He'd get up when he felt like it. I took a quick shower, dried my hair, pulled it into a neat bun, and put on a light face of makeup. I wasn't trying to overdo it for client meetings. I was supposed to manage the background noise, not look too fabulous. I pulled on my uniform—a pair of black pants and a black blazer with a colorful shirt. I stuck to black-on-black with a pop of color, so I always look professional. Today, it was a turquoise silk shell. On days I managed an event, I wore white. It kept things simple. I added a pair of booties, and rushed out of Darren's place as he woke.

I took the elevator down forty floors to the garage's guest parking. I had twenty minutes to bail out my car before management left a nasty letter telling me to move it. At ten, they would threaten to tow it. I was always on my way by 7:30. This morning, I headed out of the city.

I drove south on Lakeshore, hopped on The Skyway, and crossed into Indiana. I could have done this drive in my sleep. I made good time since I was going against traffic. I was alone with the semis clogging the road. I hopped off at a hamlet known as La Porte, taking the aptly named "La Porte Road" northeast, passing still, frosty fields before crossing into Michigan ten minutes later.

I arrived at Buffalo Shores. Or, as you might think about it, The Hamptons for Chicagoans. Here, we're a blessing and a curse. The people who come for summer like to light money on fire and act like asshats. The locals refer us to as FIPs. My mother would tell you that Illinois once promoted the "Friendly Illinois People" slogan to encourage tourism—FIP. People here don't mean *friendly* when they say FIP. They used a different f-word. The communities along the lake make most of their money between May and September. They love our money. They hate how annoying we are. I get it.

To be fair, I'm not *just* a FIP. I may have Illinois license plates, but my parents who live just up the road have Michigan plates. They're locals now, right? My family spent every summer in this sleepy little village. Or it was before it was transformed with million-dollar cottages. I spent every summer weekend on the beach loving the rush of waves, the feeling of sand between my toes, and the sun on my stubbornly pale skin. I never learned to tan. That was a folly.

Buffalo Shores is a town of only a few thousand people for most of the year. It grows by leaps and bounds on Memorial Day. While most the FIPS leave by Labor Day, we work here year-round. Our family business planned and orchestrated the biggest weddings, anniversaries, and parties in Greater Chicagoland. We worked with celebrities, sports stars, and debutantes. As such, many of our events took place in Michigan within forty miles of this sleepy beach town.

This summer, my mother delegated the biggest clients to me. As such, I was undertaking a massive wedding in Buffalo Shores on the Friday of Labor Day weekend. This was the biggest chance my mother ever took on an employee. Indeed, this was the summer that would test me professionally and personally. It challenged every assumption I held dear and left an indelible mark on who I was. Everyone counted on me. I couldn't fuck this up.

I stopped by the café on the hill which wound down to the dunes. I sipped my cappuccino in the beach parking lot, buying myself another few minutes. Now, it was time to find my sister.

Linnea, known as Linny, is my twin. We're fraternal twins so we don't even look alike. We get that a lot—are you sure you are twins? It annoys me, but it's better than someone asking us for a threesome after knowing us for thirty seconds. Linny is the creative one. I'm the organized one.

Linnea lived a block from the public beach, but she can walk from a private access point from her house. She owned a bungalow that was a work in progress. A client of ours offered it to her as a pocket listing. Had it made it on the MLS, she'd have been outbid by a developer. Everything in this town was bought up by Chicago real estate conglomerates. It had once been a fun, artsy community. It was now a place so laden with rentals that the whole tenor changed. I digress. Yes, I'm a little protective of its former vibe.

A teardown like Linny's would easily sell in the high 600s. People will knock them down and build some mcmansion which set to test the limits of any zoning ordinance for fifty miles. Linny is different, though. She loves old houses. She's quick to remind me that it's the oldest on the block. Over time, when she could afford it, she took on a new project. It was a labor of love, I guess? Either that, or her sexy-as-hell contractor was worth the hassle and money. Seriously, though. Her contractor was gorgeous. Ten-out-of-ten would have done him in a heartbeat.

"Hello, honey, I'm home!" I crossed over a plank of wood, entering from her back covered porch. It was the only flooring on offer.

"Oh, you got coffee. Of *course* you did!"

Linny tucked her blonde hair behind her ear and rolled her eyes.

Linny's workbag is slung over her shoulder, same as mine. The difference was she looked more put-together. I could have spent three times as much on my wardrobe than her, but she made it look nicer. How? I didn't know. Someone had to be the knock-out. It wasn't me. Linny has it all—the cornsilk blonde hair, the height, and our mom's cheekbones. I have strawberry-blonde hair, am short, and have childbearing hips. That is if you believe my nonagenarian Norwegian grandmother. Perhaps that's not a bug, it's a feature? The jury was still out.

"Ready to meet The Princes?" Linny asked.

I wasn't but I agreed. "Look, only *one* of them is a prince. The other is not."

"I'm going to call them The Princes forever," Linny announced.

We walked the plank to exit.

We approached their place. It was just up the block. We were tag teaming here, but Linny and I represent different industries. Linny ran a business handling the physical and musical moving parts. A sound and lighting engineer by training and trade, she moonlighted as an interior designer. She handled things like chairs, tables, lighting, and rogue musicians. I managed all the sobbing brides, overbearing mothers-in-law, and rogue guests. I told grooms where to stand. My brand was herding cats and making people play nice for the sake of the happy couple. Linny's brand was manufacturing a fairy tale.

Together, we planned to execute the happiest of endings for our most high-profile couple. Since they were our mother's friends, she stepped back. She worried about mixing business with friendship. Mamma may have partially brokered their deal on the house where we now wait at the gate. The Princes live in this massive glass lake house. We buzzed the gate to enter. In the driveway, there was a contrast of cars. First in the drive was a hybrid. Next to it was a Maserati. I wondered who owned which. I love to match people to their cars or dogs. Some like to observe art. I prefer to observe people in their native habitats. I find that fascinating.

A man with a ruddy complexion met us at the door. He wore shorts, slippers, and a t-shirt. He did not look especially princely. On his hip is an adorable blonde toddler eating a breakfast cookie. He looked flummoxed.

"I am so sorry we're so... chaotic. Come in, come in. The

nanny is sick. We have no childcare." He apologized before shouting, "Georgie! The wedding planners are here!"

His better half called, "What!?"

"The wedding planners! Hannah and Elisabeth's daughters!"

"Bugger! Sorry! Sorry!"

A man with dark brown hair and altogether lovely blue eyes appeared in the foyer. He wore jeans and a nice sweater with a dishrag thrown over his right shoulder. I noted that he must be left-handed. Interesting.

"Bloody hell, I am so sorry. The dishwasher is broken. Had to do the washing up by hand." He had a devastating English accent. I could listen to him talk all day.

Linny said in the most midwestern way possible, "It's no big deal. I have a little one. I get it."

Linny shares a six-year-old, Marie, with her ex-husband, Jeff. Linny and Jeff still worked together. He managed bands in the area. I didn't know how they remained copasetic. I assumed she was just more mature than me. Either way, they have an adorable, exhausting, and wonderful daughter. I am the proudest aunt on Earth and make no apologies for gushing.

"It's fine. We're here to help you. You could always reschedule and—"

The man holding the toddler cut me off. "God, no! It's not that bad if you can manage our mess and chaos."

"Our circus, our monkeys, but we are all yours. Patrick, you are being *rude*," the Brit said. "Ladies, it is so lovely to have you. I'm George—please just call me George—and this is Patrick, my fiancé. And this is little Charlotte."

Charlotte waved.

I grinned, "Oh, you're a cutie, aren't you?"

She giggled.

I said, "I'm Sanne. This is Linny."

We shook hands. George offered to make tea, which I didn't drink. However, if George offered, I had to say yes. I assumed this would be the first and only time that the son of a real-life

King made me tea. Patrick settled little Charlotte before the living room television and plied her with snacks like any good parent.

"Is she going to be in the wedding?" I asked.

"Yes," Patrick answered. "If she will manage it. She's hit or miss in performance these days."

I smiled and nodded. "Well, we will be glad to work with her. I am a hype machine with children."

Linny laughed and agreed. "She is. It's a notable talent."

George was hard at work pouring tea. "Put that on your CV, then."

I chuckled. "Oh, man, an honest job description for me would be a fun experiment."

George shrugged. "In a past life, mine, too."

George was difficult to describe. He was notable not because he was a prince. That alone was one thing. He was once Prince of Wales and heir to the throne—not just any old prince. He left his position and a long-term relationship with a woman to run off into the sunset with the ever-gorgeous Patrick Roughy. Patrick was a football—or soccer—phenom. They met years before when he played in the UK. The two were adorable together. They were practically gay icons. And, here we were, planning their wedding.

"Your mum is the absolute best. She says you are perfect dynamic duo for us."

I explained, "Our job is to make sure you are happy, and your wedding is beautiful. I have no doubt we will do that. We will help with anything you need."

Patrick smiled at George. "We will try not to be too high maintenance."

"It is nothing we have not seen before."

"Trust us... we have witnessed things you would not believe. We joke we should write a memoir," Linny said.

"But we have signed NDAs so that seems impossible. This is all sealed—under lock and key."

Linny's joke could have landed poorly. I saved it. Or, rather, they didn't even bat an eye at the joke. They were altogether different than I expected. The Princes were as attractive as I assumed. However, they were just so… normal. I sipped tea, a beverage I still loathe, and ran through the lead-up event must-haves.

"Well, for the stag, it's just my cousin and brother throwing it. No need to do anything."

That was good. I didn't do bachelor or bachelorette parties as a rule.

Patrick looked unamused. "Two straight guys throwing a gay bachelor party. It's… I want nothing to do with it. And I'm the one who spends all day around a bunch of straight men grunting and punching one another for fun."

"You can't decline can you, Pat?"

Patrick sighed. "Whatever, Georgie. It's not like they are holding a fucking gun to your head. I am saying we bring in Natalie because she can throw a party."

"Natalie is… your sister?" I tried to keep up.

George nodded. "But she's so busy… I dunno. She could keep them on their toes. I will get you her team's info either way, Sanne. You'll need her private secretary's contact information along with that of my parents'. My mother said her staff would work as point of contact for both my father and her."

"Oh, sure." I smiled.

The Queen's team? That would be a dream!

I presented options as to cadence of meetings. Most couples didn't want a weekly meeting. However, George insisted he did. I didn't tell him no. I saw from Patrick's eye-rolling he wanted nothing to do with planning. I would need to mind George. Patrick was the type of groom you told to show up, wear this, and he obeyed. Most grooms were like that. George, however, had *opinions*. It was fine. I planned enough weddings where both grooms had *opinions* to prefer one being the primary point of contact. Besides, George didn't scream "diva", nor did he treat us like servants. That also surprised me.

I scheduled our next two meetings. I was about to ask George if he got my invites when I became very distracted. A shirtless man wandered into the dining room in stocking feet wearing a pair of tight pants. He sipped loudly out of a Gatorade bottle. He had gorgeous abs that didn't quit, broad shoulders, and that little v-thing that drives all women crazy at the end of a man's torso. He was sexy as hell and just… standing there. I tried hard not to look, but I was confused. Why was he here? Also, were those *riding* breeches? If so, it made sense. They left little to the imagination. Again, I was not complaining, but this was distracting.

"Do you mind?" George asked, annoyed.

"What? Sorry, I didn't realize we had guests," the man said, breathless after gulping down half a Gatorade.

"We have guests, yes?"

"Ladies, this is George's brother, Paul. Paul, these are the planners—Sanne and Linnea."

"Oh, the lesbians?" Paul asked.

I made a face. *The Lesbians? Who the hell was this asshole?*

"We're not actually," I said, voice hot.

He didn't get my tone, responding in the most adorable accent, "Oh, well, my brother said you were lesbians—the planners were."

"No. That would be our mothers. We are twins," I said.

Linny kicked me under the table. She was telling me to stop. I didn't mind her.

"You don't look it—"

George groaned. "Fraternal twins. Like Natalie and I."

"You two look much closer related than these two. Oh, well. I've been to the barn. I'm knackered."

I was appalled by George's stupid, sexy excuse for a brother. He didn't say hello. He didn't say sorry. He just marched off. I expected impeccable manners. Who the hell was this oaf? Did he hate women? My distaste must have been visible because George apologized for his brother's misdeeds.

"I'm quite sorry. He doesn't mean to be rude. He's... he's just Paul."

"Is he visiting for a while?" Linny asked.

"For the summer. He's come to ride polo ponies with George and give us some help with the wedding and Charlotte," Patrick said.

"He's treating it as a bit of a gap year."

"Interesting," I said, not at all interested. Fuck this dude. What was he talking about. A *gap* year? How old was his brother. I would google it later. What I knew right then was that he had no manners. It was going to be a very, very long summer if I had to contend with Prince Asshole.

a constant
disappointment

. . .

paul

George burst into the media room where I watched a film.

"Could you maybe try *just* a bit more to be nice to guests?"

He followed with, "What on Earth are you watching?"

I paused the film. "A gritty cop drama."

"It looks dreadful."

"Not everything is sunshine and moonbeams." It *was* dreadful.

I set the remote down.

"Paul, what was that? Were you *trying* to draw attention to yourself?"

"Fuck no! Why!"

"Because you walked in wearing very little more than socks."

"I had on breeches!"

"In which literally everything was visible! Paul, I understand you are young and hot and all of that. We've all been there. God, to be twenty-five again!"

"You're only thirty, Georgie!" I laughed. "And at twenty-five you met Lucy and were practically married to her. I am not so lucky at present."

George was born fifty. We all swore by it. So was Natalie, my oldest sister. Perhaps, she was worse. She was born with indignance unmatched. She always had an axe to grind over some moral high ground. George was less ideologically annoying. However, he can be holier-than-thou in his own way.

"You cannot walk around shirtless like that. That's my only point."

"Worried that Patrick will kiss a third member of the family or—"

"I should punch you!"

I jested but it was true. When George and Pat first got together—in secret—Natalie had tried to help hide things for George by snogging Patrick very convincingly in public.

"I'm joking. I'm joking. I should have kept the shirt on. I'll grant you. I wasn't parading around expecting to impress them. I didn't expect to have two straight ladies there—are they straight?"

"Yes, I presume. One has a child but… I don't know."

"I think they were based on the way the almost-ginger one looked at me," I said.

I did think that. The little ginger was downright hostile to me, but rather gawped. I didn't mind, but wished she could be a little less rude.

"Why *were* you shirtless? Other than you've never liked wearing clothing. You are the worst one of us, Paul."

"I was so sweaty I could have rung my shirt out. I helped move hay bales. I sweated like a pig, and I threw my shirt in the wash. Honest-to-God, I didn't mean to upset you. Who are these girls anyway?"

"Our friend, Elisabeth, owns the company they work for. Her daughter—the ginger—is running point. Her name is Sanne. Her twin sister, Linnea, manages the sound and lights and that sort of thing. The reason that we can even *have* the wedding on this timeline during Patrick's by-week is because Elisabeth and her wife, Hannah, are part-owners of the hotel hosting the reception. Otherwise, this would have been impossible. Be nice to them, Paul. I will not tell you twice."

"Sorry, sorry. I will apologize if I see them again. Hopefully, I won't. I don't think the ginger liked me."

"She's fine. I think she was just confused about my half-naked brother walking around in the house—rudely and referring to them as 'the lesbians'."

"George, her mothers *are* lesbians. It cannot be offensive to simply say they are *lesbians*! Don't you want that sort of notoriety? Like, isn't that the point of pride and all of that? Aren't you always saying 'ooooh, bi-erasure is bad' and blah, blah, blah."

George looked cross, the way our father did before a blow up. I worried he was about to smack me.

"Pride is pride. Their mothers are the most important lesbians in Chicago—a lesbian power couple. Saying they are lesbians is no issue. Calling them 'the lesbians' would be as if you had a person of colour as a friend and described their family only by their race. It would reduce them to one characteristic. Do you understand why that's offensive?"

"Perhaps, yes," I conceded. "I see what you mean."

"Use your brain, Paul. Use it."

"I will... try."

I got sick of people telling me to use my brain as if I were some sort of fucking dullard. As a child, I struggled to read while the twins were academic superstars. Natalie never put down a book. She was like a Matilda-in-the-wild. George had a big brain for history and science. He had an excellent memory. I struggled with dyslexia, so all of that was difficult. The twins liked aviation and could even fly before driving a car. I struggled to pass my driver's test, embarrassingly enough, because I had ADHD and still don't function a hundred percent "right" without stimulants. No one knows any of this. It would probably bring dishonour on my family or some shit. My brain made me wildly creative in other ways, but no one saw that.

"Fine," I agreed.

There was no point in arguing with George.

"I love you, okay?" George softened. "Very much. And you're welcome to stay. I don't mean to insinuate you aren't important to Pat and I. We love you. It's just… you must be more mindful."

"Got it."

He patted my back. "And we will need you to watch Charlotte this evening, like we thought. We're going to go out to dinner with some friends at something called a Supper Club. I don't know. It seems nice."

"Oh, well have fun. I'm good. I thought we'd just order a pizza and watch kid movies until bedtime."

I was here for complicated reasons. However, I wanted to be there for Charlotte. She was a doll. People may have thought I'd rather do anything other than hang out with a two-year-old, but I loved being an uncle. Charlotte had me wrapped around her adorable, chubby fingers since the moment I met her. She was precious. I love babies—always have—but Charlotte would always be special.

I knew Patrick and George were new to the whole parenting thing. Rather, my brother may have adored children, but was green at parenting. Patrick had been a single dad with a lot of help in the UK, only to relocate back to his home country far away from Charlotte's grandparents. Charlotte's mum was not in the picture. She and Patrick never really had a *relationship* of sorts. However, she didn't want anything to do with Charlotte once Patrick came out.

George and Patrick were terrifyingly brave. I could never have done what George did—leave it all behind. Though I guess, in some way, I had. It was temporary. In theory, I could go back. George had left it all. He'd left his housing, his allowance, his cars, his plane, and his title. Yes, he had an inheritance and money from our Mum's family to rely on. He wasn't poor.

However, to go from heir to the throne to having no royal title and no livelihood was difficult. He became a stay-at-home-dad and followed Patrick across an ocean. George left his beautiful girlfriend of five years to chase this dream of who he really was. I couldn't have done it. Of course, no one had ever told me I couldn't hold my job because I liked girls.

If I thought about it too much, it made me angry. Back home, people still thought Georgie was a selfish prick. Well, a certain *group* of royalists did. They believed that Natalie bailed the family out. To her credit, she had. Natalie served dutifully even though she didn't want to be heir. She gave up her career as a decorated pilot. She left all she loved to take on the top job. I couldn't have done that, either. People didn't understand there were no sides. Natalie could have bailed us out. In the same breath, George bravely did what he thought was in the family's best interest. Both could be true.

This was why I was born third, I guess. I never had to make a tough choice. I had to step up and support Natalie. She loathed me for running off and leaving her to do the job without support. Kiersten, our youngest sister was still a baby. She wasn't ready to deploy as a working royal. But, really, am I? It's debatable. Natalie thought I left her because I'm a fuck up. The truth is far, far worse. I didn't have many other chances. My mother was able to buy me a second chance, but if our father knew what had happened, I would never see the light of day again.

So, this summer, there I was, in America. My father was none the wiser. And all because my mother loved me so much, she'd try any smoke and mirrors to spare me his wrath. I loved my mother more than anyone, so I tried to keep my nose clean. It was a small price to pay to entertain a toddler. I couldn't get into much trouble watching *Inside Out* for the thirtieth time as we ate cheese bread. Kids are magical like that. They haven't a care in the world. They are not afraid to fall or try things. They are bliss-fully unaware that the world is very limiting.

Sometimes, I envied George and Patrick. This summer, they were trying to have a baby with a surrogate. Other times, I realised how woefully unprepared I was to have a child. I'd like one someday. This summer, I was hopeful I could still find time to meet the right woman, I hoped it wouldn't go completely wrong in the process. At least, not *again* anyway.

I hoped I learned my lesson and that no one ever questioned why I was there—especially not my older sister. I worried she would be all too quick to call me on it. I couldn't blame her. Dad tasked her with the big job without backup. I never doubted she would marry and a have her own kids before too long. She needed the support. I wanted to go back and be that helper, but knew I wasn't ready.

If there is one thing I was trying to figure out, it was whether I can go back to that life. Perhaps, that seemed selfish. Like George, I worried that I was a liability to the institution. My sisters seemed better suited to making it work. It was strange how my actions impacted hundreds of years of history. And while I might have agreed that was ridiculous before George left, it seemed real now. George made immediate changes to the ways people looked at the institution—good or bad. The Firm is outdated. Natalie propped it up. Dad claimed that was *his* job to modernize it, but we knew who would bear the brunt of this change. It would be Natalie and us by proxy.

Part of me—the tiny, frightened, dutiful part of me—believed I could rush in and help Natalie. However, I was not like her. I was an unlikely choice for the military given my passivism and childhood asthma. It was a convenient out for a prince who didn't want to do any military service. I'd never been brave like my siblings. Even Kiersten was brave—racing around a jumps course astride some skyscraper-sized horse.

No, this suited me for now. It would do. Maybe it would condition me to be a better person? The goal was perspective. At least, that was what my mother and aunt said as they saved me from my father's wrath and the family from press ruination. The urge for the Firm's own self-preservation kept me safe. We buried secrets. We didn't air them. That's why George's coming out party had flown in the face of history. Living authentically was simply not done.

what you really want

. . .

sanne

I planned to return to the City for dinner with Darren and some friends after the meeting with The Princes, but first needed to drop a contract off with my mother. I drove north to Liberty Pier and ducked into my mothers' purpose-built house on the shore. Everything inside was designed to enhance views of the lake. My mother referred to it, ironically, as a *hytta*. This was a Norsk word typically attached to a tiny cottage in the woods somewhere in BFE. Much like in Michigan where everyone had a cottage "upstate", every Norwegian had a vaca-tion cottage. And like many of the "cabins" upstate, you were lucky if it had more than a wood stove. Hell, in Norway, you were lucky if there was running water.

This place was no cabin, no *hytta*. It was a grand sanctuary away from the city complete with a massive boat slip and private beach access. While we'd grown just south in a smaller house, my mothers bought a larger property when Mom retired. Mamma turned the ground floor into an office. Today, she wasn't in. I planned to leave the contract on her desk before ducking out, but I wanted to make an espresso before leaving. This would be my life for the next five and a half months.

I tamped a long shot of espresso and put it in the machine, firing up the electric kettle. I'd make an americano and hit the road. Or, anyway, that was the plan. I assumed no one was home. I was wrong. As soon as the machine kicked on, my mother appeared in the kitchen.

"So, you thought you'd steal our coffee and rush out?" she asked.

"Mom, how do you know that?"

"Because you didn't even bother to take off your coat, Sanne."

She'd caught me.

"Fine, I thought no one was home. I had to drop off the contract for the royal wedding on Mamma's desk."

I poured water in a to-go mug. This mug would live in my car for another two weeks before Mamma told me I stole all her cups. I would then clean out my car while she tsk-tsk'ed at my nomadic dumpster fire of a life.

"Ah, how was that? You like them, right?" Mom asked me.

Mom was Hannah. She was a retired, but had been one of the first out CEOs and the first out lesbian to take on the top job for a Fortune 500 company. She'd finally retired, much to Mamma's initial delight. At present, they were spending the most time together they ever had, and she was driving my Mamma, Elisabeth, crazy. Mamma was the ever-practical Norwegian. Mom's clinginess was driving Mamma up a wall. Apparently, when spouses retired, this was normal.

"Uh, yeah, whatever."

I dropped the shot into the hot water.

"You will be wired for sound." She sounded disapproving.

"Oh well, Mom."

"You didn't like them?"

"No, I do," I said. "I do. Patrick is a sweetheart. George is...

normal. He's going to be the demanding one, but he was super respectful. I was relieved."

Mom shook her head. "They're a hot mess but lovesick. And they're trying to have another baby. Heaven help them. It must be difficult to come out very publicly in your thirties. And being them… it's a lot. Mamma loves them and we can't help but handhold a bit as older gays."

I snickered. "You're old and married, Mom."

"Yes. There are worse things. Why do you look so annoyed?"

"Is it that obvious?"

"Sweetheart, you know I know you. Yes."

I groaned. "So, it's not *them*. They're adorkable. It's the stupid brother. George's dumbass brother came into our meeting —shirtless."

"What?" Mom burst into a fit of laughter.

"For real. What an asshat! He was downright rude. I got annoyed. Linny will tell you I went for him—I didn't. She's just too nice to dickheads. It's wild. George is so polite and *nice*, but his brother is some sort of meathead."

"I haven't met him."

"Well, don't. He's awful. And apparently around to 'help' so I'm not rid of him. He's here to play polo or something. Whatever. It was like he was trying to be distracting."

"Were you distracted?" she snickered.

"Fuck, Mom, no!" I lied.

Yes, of course. He was hot and shirtless. What was I supposed to do? Not at least look?

"You protest a lot."

"Look, he's hot. I am not going to deny that. But he was walking around like a total thirst trap in riding breeches. And he didn't even say hello or apologize for interrupting. Like, what the fuck?"

"Some people are weird."

"Mom, he asked if we were 'the lesbians.' George corrected him. That's what set me off."

"He has a case of foot-in-mouth-disease. Maybe he's just blunt? Mamma has the same problem."

She was not wrong. Mamma was always blunt. Some people were offended, but she was just being Scandinavian. There was no way around it. I was more like Mamma than Mom in that regard. Linny was the sweet, kind one. I was direct, not mincing words.

Mom changed the subject. "Where are you off to?"

"Home. I need to check in with a florist and make a few calls, but I figure I will do that in the car while I'm stuck on the Skyway, yeah?"

"Dangerous. You're terrible."

"I have evening plans."

"With?"

I didn't want to tell her Darren. Mom was convinced he wasn't good for me. It wasn't like he was abusive or even rude. She just thought he was a douche, for lack of a better way to put it. She'd point out our lack of obvious commitment to justify this concern. She and Mamma took this non-traditional approach to life for *years* and yet she seemed to want her straight daughters to gravitate towards a "normal" monogamous existence. Internalized patriarchy was a real bitch.

"Darren," I answered curtly.

"Uh-huh."

"Look, I know you aren't his biggest fan, but he's fine."

"Fine isn't what I want for you. I don't understand the appeal."

"Look, he's not for you, Mom. He's kind to me. He makes time for me. His parents are great. They are *normal*. Do you know how hard it is to find normal parents?"

"Are we normal?"

"Okay, maybe not to *some* people, but I think so. I meant parents who aren't fucking nightmares. He's not hideous. He has a job."

"Don't settle. I think straight women are conditioned to settle. You'll settle with him."

"Mom, he's perfectly fine. I like him. I do."

"You've been with him a year and you don't *love* him?"

"That's normal."

"Normal, normal, normal with you! Is it normal?"

"I think it is."

"I knew I loved your mother the day I met her. I told her weeks later. I think if you aren't sure now, it's a wasted effort."

"You two are a walking stereotype. She basically moved into your place two weeks later."

Mom let out a laugh. "That's fair. I wouldn't change it, though. She makes my life better. I knew it from the day I met her. She's too good for me. That's what you need. You need someone like that. Really, sweetheart, as ambitious as you are, I think you need to find a man who feels *you* are too good for him. Darren sees you like a trophy."

"There is nothing about me that is a trophy," I said in protest.

"Oh, honey, that isn't true."

"You're my Mom. You have to say that."

"Practice some self-love!"

"Mamma's new age shit is getting to you, Mom."

"Look, I'm not about to go out and buy a fucking salt lamp or climb into a sensory deprivation pool, but manifesting self-love can be good. The world tells us to make ourselves to smaller, to pick our bodies apart, and to compare ourselves to one another. I gave up on that shit years ago. An ambitious woman must set it aside. Harden up. Make choices because they allow you to be a better version of you. Put yourself first. At this point in your life, you must be ruthlessly protective of yourself and your aspirations. You have the drive. I don't want to see you lose that fire."

Her words were sweet, but difficult to accept. I knew Mom was right. She had been through a lot. She'd faced so much discrimination. When I was a little girl, I thought she was superwoman. She had to throw elbows to get a seat at the table. She refused to let people tear her down. She walked so I could run.

"Thanks," I said.

"You are beautiful—inside and out. Anyone in their right mind should appreciate that about you. Yes, I'm your mom, but I speak the truth. Women like us—those who want to take over the world—they must be strong and ignore what society wants them to think. You're beautiful. You're enough. Own that shit. Don't let it eat you alive. Don't minimize your talents."

"Okay."

"Make this the best event you've ever done," Mom said. "And brush up your CV. It's time for you to jump."

"Mamma needs me—"

"The world needs you. You're too talented to waste away as a wedding planner the rest of your life. Not that I don't think your mother is fabulous at it, but you're a PR rep deep down. You want to solve the world's problems. You could be an amazing chief of staff or chief strategist. Mamma loves working with brides and designers. That is not what fills your cup, sweetie. Be honest. You can run this thing and get any job you want. Don't settle."

Mom's words hit me hard. She was right. It was what I trained for, what I wanted. As a child, when people asked what I wanted to be when I grew up, I said the President's Chief of Staff. It was true. I did. I managed many-a-crisis. I lived for it. I was excellent at my job. I thought for sure Mamma would ask me to take over the business. She was near retirement now. Did I want that, though? Was that what was best for me? I wasn't sure I was ready to jump.

I gave Mom a hug and left. I drove back to the city thinking about what I really wanted. Could I close this chapter? I loved working with Mamma. I lived to be with my family. Putting myself out there for the big job was scary. It wasn't the fear of rejection. It was the fear of failure. Was I ready to move far away from my family with no support system? Maybe I could take a middle-way approach. I could take a bigger job but stay in Chicago. It might not be the dream job I was looking for—yet. But it would get me to that job. And, perhaps by then I'd have a husband. Maybe someday kids? I wasn't sold on that yet. I was open to it in a few years.

I worried that by the time I made a choice, I'd be past the age of having it all. Maybe Mom knew something I didn't? It was possible. You could say many things about my mothers, but they knew us. They would have done anything for us. They *did* do anything for us. To get us, they went through hell—insemination, legal issues, discrimination in the courts. They fought so hard. I had it easy in comparison. Maybe they were worried I'd never have it all if I didn't leap? Or, maybe, it was because they worried it would take me forever to make up my mind. I hated to admit I was the baby bird needing a push.

I returned home, calling back a few clients who had weddings that weekend. I would need to be two places in once, delegating things to my assistant on Friday night. I would have one small wedding at the Cultural Center and one rehearsal at the planetarium going at the same time. I'd manage, though. My clients would be happy. I knew it would work out.

Work was never an issue for me. I made the impossible possible. It was my love life that needed to get its shit together. What did I want? Was I really settling with Darren? I still liked him a lot. Maybe I just was incapable of loving anyone? I wasn't one of those lovesick girls who dropped everything for a man. He'd never asked me to do that. But was that good? Should I have been willing to give that to someone if I was going to have a life with someone? It was all so confusing. I'd deal with it later.

transatlantic complications

. . .

paul

"Turn that off!" George demanded before flopping on the couch.

I flipped off the telly and looked at him. He was bereft. We were in the house alone. This vent came courtesy of Patrick being at a night scrimmage. His coach was a pain in the arse, from what I could gather. In the UK, no one would have shown up. Americans were odd. It was quiet. Charlotte was asleep. I'd been there in their living room in the beautiful high-rise they occupied. I was enjoying a pirated copy of a show on the BBC not yet in the US.

"Yes, brother?" I asked, kissing my evening goodbye. "What is the news at home?"

"How did you know what was going on at home? Is it already all over the news?"

"I don't know, honestly. I just assumed. Your cadence of speaking to one of us versus one of the Americans is different. I just assumed. You were in proper George mode on the phone."

"Ah, alright. It was Mum. She was trying to spare me."

"From what?" I took the bait.

I wanted to get this over with.

George didn't answer. He hopped up, looking flustered and went to the liquor cabinet. He returned with two glasses and a bottle of expensive bourbon from Mum's family distillery. We were forever spoiled. We would be here a while. I was fine talking about feelings, but George was awkward. He only ever talked to Natalie about that stuff. I was his second choice on this evening—by a mile.

"He's done it," George took a swig.

He didn't pour one for me. I had to do that much.

"Who? Can you explain it, Georgie?"

"Winston. He's married her, damn it! They surprised everyone. And the news will be announced next weekend, so they have time to tell her family."

"What? How?"

"They got married at some little place near their house—just Natalie, Ed, the cousins, Auntie Rita, and Uncle Bruno," George said.

"He married Lucy?"

"Can't say shit about her now. Oh, she's the Countess. She's my cousin-by-marriage. How fucked is this?"

George was licking his wounds. I still didn't quite understand why he even cared. Lucy was his ex. They'd been nearly engaged when he broke it off and ran away with Patrick. Lucy, jilted, moved in with a friend—our second-cousin Winston. Lucy and Winston got together by some twist of fate and became engaged quickly. I was happy for Winston. He was, like me, a bit of an oddball. She took care of him. The rest of the family was happy. They couldn't see the problem. George saw it as an attack. She had been *his*. Winston was in *his* territory.

"George, she's allowed to marry someone else. Be happy for Winston. He loves her. Besides, if you bring this up to Patrick, he'll be cross."

"I'm aware. I'm not upset with Lucy. I'm upset with Winston."

"Winston has a right to marry Lucy as much as anyone. *You* left her. Let it go. This is only going to end up going poorly for you across the board."

George refilled his glass. *Oh, here we go!*

"Natalie was there," George said, astonished. "Natalie was one of the witnesses. She got invited. Can you believe that?"

I couldn't stifle a laugh. "Were you offended to not be invited?"

"I feel betrayed."

"Natalie has never betrayed any one of us. Lucy is her personal secretary. She's also Natalie's best mate—"

"She's *my* best friend. Natalie is *my* best mate!"

I wasn't about to argue with George. "She's Natalie's best *girl*friend."

"She chose Lucy over me."

"George, that's ridiculous. She supported her friend. I won't remind you of all Natalie has done for you out of love. I would say Natalie is owed a benefit of the doubt here. This isn't an act of malice. She supported Lucy and Winston. Winston and Ed are close. Of course, he was going to support his friends, too."

"Fucking Ed," George scoffed.

Ed was Natalie's serious boyfriend.

"You like Ed! Patrick loves him! I have never heard you say a word against the man. Stop. Natalie loves him. Have we ever seen her like this?"

"She's lovesick. It bothers me."

"So are you. Fuck off, Georgie."

"Patrick only likes him because they're both athletes—"

"You *both* like Ed. Stop being a petty tosser, Georgie. Really."

George let out an exasperated groan and fell back on the couch, as if giving up.

"George, it's time to take the high road."

"Why did they even get married? Could they not wait?"

"Because maybe they didn't want to involve Winston's dad? Or complicate matters for everyone? Or even *you*. You know they both care about you, right? Maybe it was to not distract from Gerry and Sheena's wedding?"

Gerry was Winston's younger brother. He and George had been best mates growing up. He was set to marry Sheena, his long-time girlfriend, in May. It was going to be the biggest wedding of the British social season. George and I were serving as attendants.

"No, I think it is the opposite."

"Could he have knocked her up?" I asked.

George sat back up in a flash and said, "It must be that! Oh, of course, they *would* be breeders! Fuck them!"

"George, you and Patrick have a surrogate."

"It's not the same. He'd be so lucky to get her pregnant and rush to marry her, wouldn't he? Or maybe *she* planned it?"

"Or maybe they just wanted to have a baby?"

"Impossible."

"Lucy adores kids. She's always wanted kids," I pointed out. "That's unfair. Look, if she *did* fall pregnant, it's neither your problem nor is it good to curse them for it. Just take the fucking high road and move on, mate."

"I don't like it when you sound like Mum."

I chuckled. "Sorry. What did she tell you?"

"In the sweetest American way possible, she told me to calm the fuck down."

That sounded about right. Mum was raised in the States. She was Welsh by birth, but her mannerisms were all American. She had adjusted to life in the UK but retained many Americanisms. The attraction to Americans was a curse for George. Lucy had been born a stone's throw from where we now sat. Patrick was Californian by birth. Both had moved to the UK as teenagers— Lucy to go to uni, Patrick to play in the Champion's League. Lucy had stayed on to work for our Mum. That was how George met her and how all of us became close to her.

"She is right," I said.

"I cannot believe everyone is just siding with him. Gerry isn't responding to my text—"

"You would think that Gerry would choose you over his brother? Especially given that Sheena and Lucy are terribly close? He'd be stupid unless he wanted to anger his mother, brother, and future wife."

"Perhaps, you're right."

"I am, brother. I can assure you."

"Supposedly, they are coming to Chicago to tell her parents. Should we invite them round? Take them to dinner?"

"Are you going to be a knob and get into a shouting match like you did at Christmas?"

George and Winston nearly came to blows before George apologised to Lucy. George accused Lucy of having loud sex *at* him. It was mortifying. Their parents were unimpressed. George skated on thin ice for a bit. Our mum adored Lucy and our dad hated such behaviour.

"No," George said. "I will be on my best behaviour."

"You could text them both a congratulations. That would go a long way. If they respond—and only if—invite them out to dinner. Not here. Neutral territory. I guarantee Winston and Lucy will avoid you like the plague if you have them here. What will Patrick think about this?"

"He will think I'm being a grown up. He would support it."

"Well, you'll earn brownie points, then, right?"

"Correct. Yes. That is a good idea."

I held out my hand. "Give me your mobile."

George passed it over. "How do you know my passcode?"

"It's Charlotte's birthday. You and Patrick have the same passcode. It's aggressively endearing."

I added Winston and Lucy to a group message thread.

I typed, not trusting my brother on his third large pour, to handle this. He'd have done the same for me.

> Sorry for texting so late. Hope you're not minding your phones at all. Mum told me about the good news. Wanted to wish you a congrats. Cheers!

Knowing George used as many emoji as an elderly woman with her first smartphone, I added a champagne bottle and confetti before sending. I handed back the mobile.

"Leave it, alright?"

"Fine, fine," George agreed, grudgingly. "What are they up to?"

I raised my eyebrows. "You want specifics? Probably having lots of sex."

"Ugh! That is not what I wanted you to say!"

"George, what do you want me to fucking say? You are rubbish at this. Just admit it makes you feel insecure to see her move on. Admit it and let it go."

"I'm cross with Winston—"

"No, you're not. I mean, yes, you're being a territorial prick. I'll grant you that. Still, there's more there. You feel like she moved on because she never actually loved you or whatever."

"I hate talking about my feelings."

"I know," I chuckled.

He didn't. He was dreadful at it.

"This is why I call Natalie. Why isn't she picking up?"

"Well, It's five AM there, George. Even she is not up that early. Also, she's probably shagging Ed if she *is* awake. That outranks you."

"God, I don't want to think about it. What does she see in him?"

"That he loves her?"

"I think she finds him hot."

I laughed and shook my head.

"Well, he is. The man is beautiful. I hate her a little. I mean, so is Patrick."

"You share a type. She fancied Patrick before she knew, didn't she?"

"Fuck. Off."

"You hate when we remind you of it, huh?"

George glared.

"Alright, calm down, Georgie."

"Paul, you are insufferable sometimes. I am still cross."

"Be cross, but don't let Patrick know about it. He'll be offended and it will lead to a pointless, idiotic row over Lucy that will make him feel insecure. For Patrick's sake, take the high road."

George looked dissatisfied with my retort.

"You love him, don't you? You blew up your entire life for him. You caused a hell of a scandal. All because you couldn't imagine a life without him. Winston and Lucy tempted the same fate. Just appreciate the beauty of the both of you finding someone to build a life with."

"But then did it mean anything?"

Ah, *that* was the real George coming through. Gone was his macho tirade. He was sad and vulnerable. I trod carefully.

"It did. Georgie, you two grew up together. You taught one another a lot. Does every relationship have to end in a lifetime of happiness to mean something? Don't some just… teach you about life?"

George shrugged. "I only ever loved her and Patrick. And often at the same time, sadly."

"And now?"

"Nothing."

"Then let it go, brother."

"I failed."

"You thrived despite difficulty. I wouldn't have the bullocks to do what you did. You loved her enough to let her go. You were honest with yourself and everyone. I would have just married her and settled."

"Is that the plan?"

"No," I replied.

"Is that what happened with Katrine?" George asked.

I sat, nervous to speak.

"I loved her. She didn't love me," I answered. "And it didn't work out."

"Is that what happened? You never speak—"

"It's complicated." I felt my throat close.

George didn't want to talk about it anymore than I did. He let it go.

"Well, don't settle. It's not fair to you or the person you'd settle with. You're right. It was brave. Lucy is a sweet woman, though. I loved her enough to let her be. I suppose you are right. I should let her be happy."

"I love you, George," I said. "I know it's complicated but in ten years, this all won't matter. You'll have a house full of little ones and not care."

George smiled. "I hope you're right."

life choices

. . .

sanne

My sister called, panicked on a Friday morning in April. She had no one to pick up Marie from school. She was in St. Joe dealing with a "wedding emergency" with an angry mother-in-law who was about to kill a deal with a DJ. This would be very expensive and complicated for us. Linny could not let this old bitch ruin a long-time vendor relationship. I was just as close—at a venue in Chesterton doing a final walkthrough setting up an anniversary party the next day. It was tight, but I thought I could make it to Michigan in time. Thankfully, this was a slow weekend.

I wrapped things up, hopped in my car, and sped north on 94 until I hit the exit. I dropped by to grab Marie in the nick of time. She was so excited to see me. The weather was good. It was a sunny afternoon and warm enough to sit outside. I decided to do the cool aunt thing and take her for ice cream. The best spot on Earth, as far as I was concerned, was Moo's. The place was pure kitsch—cows wherever you looked. She got a Midwestern delicacy, Blue Moon. I got grasshopper.

We sat on the patio, watching traffic. It was slow and quiet. I figured I might take her for dinner. Why waste the weather? It was good bonding time. She was so cool, I thought. Her big red sunglasses were a *statement* piece. They perfectly matched her little smock dress and hair bows which held back her poofs. Her mother could do her hair. I always fucked it up. Natural Black hair texture was something I still hadn't mastered as an auntie.

"When do you think Berman's will open?" she asked.

"Soon, I think."

Berman's is another institution. We townies would be able to get in for a couple weeks to enjoy the world's best burger before the FIP hordes arrived. I relished the idea. It made me want a burger.

"Can we go on a date there?" she asked.

"Of *course*. Twist my arm, kiddo."

We watched as a Mercedes G pulled into the parking lot. Illinois plates. A FIP for sure! Again, I may have had Illinois plates, but I refused to be considered one. It was a state of mind, and I wasn't in it.

"Look at that big truck!" Marie pointed out a bright red classic driving by.

"That's beautiful! What a cool truck."

The kid loved classic cars. She'd pled with me to take her to a car show last summer. I wondered if she might be a bit of a car collector someday.

I turned back to my ice cream. I neared the cone. My favorite thing was to get to the bottom and discover a big cookie piece there. You never knew if it would happen but hope sprung eternal. As I looked up, preoccupied by this dream scenario, I met the gaze of the Mercedes's occupant. *Oh, boy!*

At first, I thought it was just any blonde man toting a toddler. Instead, it was The Frog. At least, that was what I was calling him in my mind now. He was more frog than frog prince. What was he doing here? Did he have nothing better to do? I prayed we didn't have to sit with him. God, Marie was taking forever! We'd be here an eternity! I worried.

Paul held little Charlotte's hand and put his free hand over his eyes to cut the glare, "Is that you Sanne? It's Sanne isn't it?"

I was hoping we could ignore one another like Scandinavians on vacation. It was like we'd seen our neighbor while on a trip, but we mutually agreed to say nothing. No. He was painfully British. We were about to have an *exchange*. Besides, Marie was a friendly person. We were gonna be here awhile.

"It's me," I said. "Just getting a cone."

"We were going to do the same. Your Mum recommended it to George. He swears by it. They had to deal with something in the city. So, I've got the monkey today."

"Well, it's a lovely day for some ice cream," I said politely.

Awkward as ever, Paul left. He and Charlotte ordered ice cream while Marie interrogated me.

"Who is he?"

"He is a brother of a client," I answered. "Your Mom and are working on a wedding for his brother."

"Oh, cool."

The two returned and sat next to us.

"Hi, I'm Marie!" my little charge said.

She approached with her ice cream.

"Marie, don't be rude—"

"No, it's fine," Paul said. "I'm Paul."

"I Char-wotte," the little one announced in a precious baby voice.

"Nice to meet you," Marie said, as if an official village greeter. "Sanne is my aunt."

"I figured. I'm Charlotte's uncle."

"It's fun to have an aunt. I don't have any uncles. Aunt Sanne isn't married. My mom says that will happen when pigs fly," Marie said.

I could have died of embarrassment. I was about to lose it.

I tried to keep my voice together. "Marie, please. Paul doesn't care—"

Paul chuckled. "Kids say the silliest things. It's alright. My siblings and parents would say the same about me, kiddo."

Marie cocked her head. "You talk funny."

"Marie, you're being rude!" I was mortified.

Paul didn't react in anger. "I'm aware. Did you know that my mum sounds like you? And my dad sounds like me? I'm from the UK. That's across an ocean."

"Why are you here? Did you move?"

"Just for the summer," he answered.

I am surprised that, unlike with adults, Paul is sweet with kids. Maybe that's because that's where his maturity level lies?

"My brother moved to America to marry his fiancé. His fiancé, Patrick, is American. They live here now," Paul said. "I'm just helping out with my niece and lazing about a bit. Long story. Boring story. Riding horses mostly."

"Horses? My aunt rides horses!"

I corrected her, "I *rode* horses. Not much anymore."

"What, really?" Paul looked downright ecstatic to talk about horses.

God, help me!

"I used to show hunters. It's nothing, really. I swear."

"So then you're one of those Hunter Princesses my mother talks about?"

I made a face. I wanted to tell him to fuck off.

"I would not refer to myself as a *princess*. That's a pejorative term that jumpers and eventers use against us."

"Apologies," Paul said. "It doesn't mean much abroad since hunting is a sport and all. Mum *was* one."

"Riding is a sport. I could take pot-shots at polo for being ridiculous, I'm sure," I said, my disdain all too obvious.

"Oh, I didn't mean to insinuate it was not. Just that hunting is... different. It's not pretty and for shows. That's all. At least, that is as my mum would say."

I back off.

"Have you ever even seen a polo match?" Paul asked.

I replied, "Um, no. I haven't."

"You should come. We've got a match Sunday." Paul assumed I have an interest in seeing him ride around on a stupid polo pony.

"Yeah, I dunno. Weekends for me are complicated and Sundays are my only day off—"

"It's fun. Free booze and food. I promise. Weather will be brilliant. Hand me your phone." Paul motioned at me.

"Uh… why?"

"Just let me give you my number."

Marie stared at me now. I couldn't be rude.

"Sure," I digressed. "I don't think it will text the UK."

"I have an American number, Sanne," Paul said. "Calm down."

He put in the number and handed it back.

It's Pa

There was the text. I wanted to block him. Perhaps, I would? Was that professional? Probably not. Instead, I gave him a half-hearted thumbs up.

"I'll shoot you some deets," Paul said.

Deets? God, that was *cringe!*

I nodded as Marie announced she was done with her ice cream. Meanwhile, Charlotte spilled a bunch of hers down the front of her dress.

"Well, bugger." Paul realized he hadn't grabbed enough napkins.

"Rookie mistake." I bailed him out with a stack I grabbed.

"Cheers. Saved me."

"That's basically my job," I joked. I sucked down the rest of the cone. *No cookie, damn it!*

"Well, perhaps you are my white knight, then?" Paul asked.

"Unlikely," I said.

If that was his attempt at a line, it was weak sauce.

We left, his gaze making me uncomfortable. Paul was so presumptive. Yes, of course, I would fall all over myself for some thirst trap prince. I resisted the urge to clap back with some awesome comeback here. Let's face it, though, I had nothing. Instead, I took the kid to the beach, then dinner at an Italian place, and tucked her into bed with a book. No comebacks, no thinking about *him. He will not take up room in my mind, damn it.* As I wondered if I would ever get home, my sister appeared with an entire pizza. Time for second dinner.

"Just stay here, Sanne," she said. "I know you. You've got a dress in your car."

It was true. Thanks to my uniform, everything matched. I always had a pair of black shoes, dress, and suit in the car. It was a must in my business.

"I'll make you breakfast," she mentioned.

"Fine, fine," I agreed. "Twist my arm."

"How was she? You're amazing for coming to my rescue."

"Marie was great." I looked at my phone as it buzzed on the coffee table. I set my plate down and picked it up. It was a text from Paul.

> Hey. Deets are match starts at noon. Most people get there around eleven for brunch. George and Patrick would love to see you. Feel free to bring a couple people. Kids are welcome. Your niece is lovely.

At least he had one thing right. My face pulled into a scowl. Linny looked from her own phone.

"What?"

"Oh, just this."

I slid my phone over to her.

"Who is The Frog?"

I forgot that I had changed his contact info to that in a fit of rage just seeing his stupid "hi" on my phone.

"Paul," I said. "God, he's so annoying."

"How did Paul get your number? Did George—"

"No. I gave it to him."

She shot me a look like, "Oh really?"

"Don't do that."

"Do what?"

"This thing you do? Oh, you're judging me. Stop it!"

Linny giggled. "Tell me what happened and I will tell you why you should judge *me*. Alright?"

"Tell me yours first."

"I fucked Jeff."

"Okay, that is worse." Fucking your ex-husband outranked all things in my book.

"See, now you have a face of judgement. Look, it happens, okay?"

"No, it should *not*. And this… this is not a *thing* and it's not happening. It wasn't a romantic thing. He was inviting us to a polo match—"

"He was inviting *you* to a polo match. Oh, yes, that sounds totally platonic."

"There is nothing romantic about a polo match."

"Have you ever been to one?"

"No."

"Exactly."

"I like horses. I think he was just being nice. Your child—"

"Oh, don't blame Marie for this, girl. He's hot. Go for it."

"He's a client. We aren't supposed to fuck clients."

Linny snickered. "Maybe you don't. Also, he's not the client. His brother is. I don't think you're planning on sleeping with George?"

"George seems more appealing," I joked.

"Oh stop it. The man is a snack. He's a whole fucking meal. If he'd expressed interest in me, I might not have fucked Jeff. I was so horny."

"I don't need to get laid. And you're forgetting that I have a boyfriend—"

"Uh-huh. But that wasn't the first reason you told me that you weren't going to go."

"Why does everyone think Darren is dunzo?"

"Because, Sanne, you don't even talk about him—"

"You all hate him—"

"We don't hate him!"

I say, "Fine. Whatever."

"It's dead as can be, isn't it?"

I let out a long sigh, "I hate it when you do this."

"You know I am right."

"So smug. And regardless of what happens with Darren or doesn't, I'm not fucking Paul. I'd rather light myself on fire in a parking lot," I say.

the boyfriend

· · ·

paul

I wasn't sure that Sanne would come to our match. I wasn't even sure why the hell I invited her. Did I even like her as a person? Was this a sticky situation to get myself in? What the hell was I doing? To be honest, I had no interest in hopping into bed with the wedding planner. She didn't even seem to particularly like me. Maybe I read the wrong thing into that. She was a bit curt. I couldn't understand her. I was trying, as George said. It was polite to invite an uninitiated horse person to a polo match.

George and Patrick immediately suspected my motives. They were sure I wanted to chat her up. No matter what I said, they refused to believe my intentions were pure. George reminded me that if I fucked things up with the planners, he'd have my head and Dad would tan my hide. That was accurate. I had no intention of doing that. I was skating on thin ice as it was. I needed to win over Miss Whatever Her Name Was. Damn, I didn't even know *what* her last name was.

To my surprise, Sanne showed up. I spotted her talking to Patrick as George as I warmed up. Maybe she didn't hate me?

Maybe there was hope in the end? The real question was still what I was *doing*? I wasn't even sure if I liked her, let alone wanted to impress her. Still, I found myself riding over to the side-lines to say hello to Patrick and get a word in. I tried to play it cool.

"Can I get a water?" I asked Patrick. "Or, as you say, *wadder*."

"Stop it." Patrick chuckled and handed me a water. "You're being rude."

"Shit," I opened the bottle, looking at Sanne as if she weren't the entire reason I'd approached. "You came?"

"I didn't want to be rude. I was in town," she was even toned.

There was not an *ounce* of flirtation there. That was good, right? I was *not* trying to chat her up.

"Cool, cool," I stammered awkwardly. "Brilliant."

We stood around. I drank way too much water. It was dreadful. I could be awkward. I wasn't like George. He could turn the conversation around to himself in a self-deprecating manner. I had gotten my father's unique ability to seize up when I should have been charming. I always wondered how my father managed to land my mother when he melted down at the smallest hint of awkward. Mum carried him in social situations. Together, they were flawless. Apart, he was a dork. I suppose on this day I was, too. *Bugger!*

To make matters worse, a man walked up beside her. He appeared to *know* Sanne.

"The donuts are bomb," he said.

I waited for her to introduce me. I waited for her to give him some sort of title. However, Sanne looked genuinely disinterested. It was now frustrating me. Women didn't usually flat out *ignore* me. It stung. I must have indicated I was displeased in some way because Patrick saved me.

"I am being rude, right?" Patrick sounded nervous. "I should introduce you. This is Sanne's boyfriend, Darren. Darren, this is Paul, my future brother-in-law."

Boyfriend. Brilliant! Okay, well at least I knew where I stood. I tried not to pull a face. *Don't pull a face, don't pull a face.* I could not have been entirely successful given Patrick's expression. I had to muster politeness. It wasn't *her* fault she had a boyfriend.

"Nice to meet you," I said. "I didn't realise you had a boyfriend, Sanne."

I added that last bit to make it sound like she might have been into me and, through a lie of omission, led me to believe otherwise. That provoked a response from Darren. My comment landed. Such strategy wasn't lost in translation in the Atlantic.

"For about a year, actually," Darren said.

He shuffled nervously, putting his hand around her waist in a pathetic act of ownership.

I didn't know why that bothered me so much. Obviously, I felt she was wasted on this wanker. She was too attractive for him. Perhaps her sister was the real stunner. She was taller and perhaps more exciting to look at, but Sanne grew on me. She was the girl next door. Darren was too short. I didn't like that for her. And while he was probably wealthy, given the Rolex on his wrist, his whole getup screamed "nouveaux riche". George would have pointed this out if he were here.

As if he could sense I was about to cause a kerfuffle, my dear brother arrived. George pulled his mare up to close to mine. My horse made it clear she was displeased by pinning her ears and biting. George moved his out of the way while saying a quick hello to Sanne.

"She's in heat. She'll kick," I warned.

"Oh, really?" Darren found that funny.

"No, I'm serious," I said. "She's a real cow when she's in heat."

"That's why Billy was a nightmare on the damn float this morning. That would have been a lovely detail to know before I dealt with him or put him where I did," George groaned.

"You compete stallions?" Sanne asked, confused.

"No. Well, Billy isn't anymore," George said. "He's just a

dickhead who was a stud for a bit. He was bellowing like he was about to cover a line of mares this morning. I had to keep smacking him. Mouthy, too."

"Feeling his oats," Sanne laughed.

"I don't pretend to understand any of that," Patrick shook his head.

"George," Sanne sounded sweet suddenly. "This is my boyfriend, Darren. Darren, this is George."

"So nice to meet you," Darren shot me a *look* again.

What the fuck was this guy's problem? What was his damage? I dared interact with Sanne. But it was okay, George was fine. Darren was threatened.

"Paul, we should keep moving. Bets is falling asleep." His horse looked about ready to take a nap.

I mustered my sweetest, most welcoming tone, "Fine, fine. Glad you all came! Enjoy the match."

We trotted off.

George asked, "You're the welcome wagon now?"

"Fuck off, Georgie!"

"What. I'm not supposed to say anything!? You *invited* her. She brought a boyfriend. Did you think to ask if she had one? If not, joke's on you."

"She never mentioned it. Women usually mention it if they assume you are inviting them anywhere that might be a date."

"But you said, 'Oh, George, this isn't a date! I was just being polite.' Your internal meltdown suggests otherwise."

"I am not melting down internally, asshole."

"You look like Dad when he must deal with Ed. It's a red flag."

I snickered.

"I am serious. Step away from her."

"I am not stepping towards her. It's clear she has a boyfriend."

Our horses continued on, plodding away. The wheels turned in my head.

"But what if he's just a plant? What if she is trying to provoke me?"

"What?" George laughed.

"As in he's her fake boyfriend and she asked him to attend because she doesn't want me to know she does not have a boyfriend. She's trying to get a rise out of me. I won't let her have one."

George shook his head. "You think I was delusional about Lucy? This is downright ridiculous. She's already gotten a rise out you. What is a fake boyfriend?"

"It's a trope. A romance trope. Kiersten's stupid books."

"You want her."

"Well, because I can't have her," I said.

"So you *do* want her?"

"She's attractive, yeah?"

"You called her stumpy when we badgered you."

"You made good points. That she has nice tits and is not stumpy."

"Yes, Patrick even acknowledged that much," George said.

He continued as we walked our horses. "Because she does. But Jesus fucking Christ, Paul, leave it be. He's not a fake boyfriend she's brought to provoke you into confessing your love for her. Why you watch those dreadful movies and read those stupid books—"

"I don't!" I would not admit to reading a few of my sister's romance novels out of boredom while on holiday. This trope was dangerously addictive. I would not say I liked them, but would concede they were entertaining.

"Don't lie. You love a rom-com. You will willingly watch them on film."

"I can enjoy a feel-good story, can I not?"

"You're the straight one!"

"I like a cheesy movie every once in a while."

"You and Patrick are terrible," George groaned. "I blame

Kiersten's bad taste and the fact that both of you are suggestible."

"I am not!"

"Uh-huh. Get your head in the game, bruv." He picked up a canter and left me in the dust.

Now, I am left wondering what to think. I fancy her. I can't deny that any longer. Yes, she is attractive. She has nice tits. I'd not mind seeing her naked. However, I could say that for so many women—women who weren't being absolute cows over everything. Sanne thought she was too good for me. Or, alternatively, she was playing hard-to-get with this boob at her side.

That had to be it! I was only attracted to what I couldn't have. That was it! Well, I wasn't going to fall for it. She was pretty enough but not worth it. I would not give her the satisfaction of seeing me wind up. Instead, I would just play the absolute best game of polo.

Thankfully, we were the ringers, because as we came up on chukka three, I was playing one of the *worst* games of my life. I thought George might take me off my horse as if we were jousting. He yelled at me more than he worked *with* me. I loathed it when he outshone me so much. He was the better player. I was lazy and not competitive. I played for fun. George was out for blood like it was his birth right. In a way, it was. Today, though, I played lousy.

George rode up to me during the cool down. "Next time don't invite a girl in hopes to impress her without asking if she's attached. Get out of your damn head."

"It has nothing to do with her—"

George rolled his eyes. "Bull. Fucking. Shit."

Irritated, I hand my horse to a groom before grabbing a beer. Time to drown my sorrows and chat up a girl who *was* available just to prove to George that I was resilient and just having a shit day. I was determined to pull this day out of the bin if it killed me. I could have a good time despite Sanne. I would not let her win.

the glass slipper

. . .

sanne

I tried keeping up with Darren. He made friends with some guy named Raul who liked talking investments. I was bored already. He'd left me in the dust. I loathed when he did this. He saw dollar signs and forgot that I wasn't a piece of furniture. I wanted to shout at him. To make matters worse, I knew no one else here but Patrick. Patrick celebrated with George. I wasn't intervening.

Worst of all, I was in the *wrong* shoes. According to a woman I met by the porta potties—*ugh*—wedges and flats were best. My heels caused me grave pain in the turf. It was a nightmare situation. My heels weren't high, but I was not the most graceful woman alive. My mother would have been fine. She would have done it in five-inch stilettos and never flinched. With my weak ankles, I struggled to keep up with my distracted boyfriend. And, as I did, I tripped.

I was mortified. I knew I was about to fall. My one shoe stopped in a mushy spot, sinking into the ground. My ankle gave out. I went face first, trying to catch myself. The last thing I thought was, *thank God I wore full-coverage panties!* They were literally about to save my ass. Then, to my surprise, someone caught me.

A guardian angel grabbed around my waist, holding me like an unruly child trying to escape. They put me right. I was down one shoe, but I hadn't gone face first into the turf. I was grateful. It turned to see who had saved me and spied The Frog pulling my shoe out of the ground.

Well, fuck.

"Your glass slipper failed you," he joked.

"That is the corniest thing anyone has ever said to me." I took my shoe out of his hand, forcefully.

We stood looking one another over. He had these beautiful blue eyes. I hated them, of course. He was so frustrating and try-hard. I wasn't falling for it. I could admit he was conventionally attractive. He was taller than I expected. It was the first time I stood in front of him. This was an observation not a judgement.

"Not even a thank you?" he asked.

"For what?" I asked.

"For saving you."

"You didn't save me—"

"I didn't? You were falling down, and I caught you," Paul protested.

We stood silent. I wanted to have a witty comeback. I was desperate to think up something. *Come on, come back, trounce him!* Paul set his jaw in this way that made him look undeniably hot. No one so insufferable deserved such a devastating jaw line.

"You may have caught me, okay?" I allowed.

"Are we also going to debate if the Earth is round?"

"What?"

"I *did* catch you, Sanne. There is no argument."

"I just… I meant like… you may have caught me, but you didn't let me finish—"

"Huh?"

God, why was I so inarticulate?

"I just… I meant like you may have caught me, but you

didn't *rescue* me. I'm not some ridiculous princess in need of rescue, thanks. Maybe that's your thing or your world but I don't do that!" I crossed my arms.

Yeah, that would do the trick!

He furrowed his brow. "I don't know of any princesses in need of rescue. My sisters can outride me, my older sister is a deadly shot, and both are braver than I am. So, if we're being serious here, I didn't think you needed actual rescue. I was making a bloody joke. You Americans don't understand proper humor."

"No, I just think you want to feel important."

"Really?" He shook his head.

"Babe!" I heard Darren's voice.

"What?" I asked, my voice hot.

I couldn't take my eyes off Paul. It was like I wanted to smite him down but could not look away.

"I'm ready to head out." Darren reached us.

"Okay, fine," I stared at Paul.

He now wiped sweat off his brow with the bottom of his shirt. His abs poked out in a distracting flash. I was sure that Darren wanted to sweep me away by this point, but it was like a trainwreck. I couldn't look away.

"Nice to meet you," Paul tried to sound cheerful. "And nice to see you, as ever, Sanne."

He was trying to kill me with kindness. I want to reply with, "Die in a ditch!" I resisted. Instead, I took Darren's hand and we left.

As we drove back to his place, Darren decided it would be a good time to have A Very Serious Conversation. I was in no mood for this, but he never read the room.

"I thought you could come on the family trip to The Bahamas," Darren said.

"In October?" I murmured, distracted.

"Yes," he answered. "Would you like to come?"

"October is... far off."

Darren nervously chuckled. "So, are you planning on ducking out? C'mon. I think we can take a trip together, Sanne."

I didn't know what to say. At this moment, I honestly *didn't* want to plan a trip with Darren. I flashed back to the conversation I had with Mom and then the one with Linnea. I shouldn't tell him that I want to go.

Instead, I said, "We can talk about it. I will check my planner and all that. Clients, you know? Why are you so keen on me coming? I'm not family—"

"Well, I was just thinking... like we could go. I mean, by then, I'd like to be engaged."

Stop the car! Let me out! Stop the car!

I didn't say anything. My silence said everything. Darren talked more to fill in the silence. This made it worse.

"Well, I love you Sanne. I think we're headed in that direction. We've been together a year. Piss or get off the pot, you know? And I know you work a lot, but if we got married, you wouldn't have to work anymore. We could have kids and you could travel whenever you wanted to—"

Had we not been on The Eisenhower, I would have jumped from the car. I wasn't sure what to say as we crawled to a stop in traffic. I wanted to climb out of his Porsche and rush up the off-ramp.

"Darren, I think that's premature. Also, I have no intention to give up work. I love working—"

"You like rushing around dealing with rich people problems? You're like a servant. That's below you, baby. You and I are both children of privilege. A pretty woman like you should be spoiled. I want to do that. I love you, like I said. You say you want to get married someday—"

"That's a hypothetical," I cut him off. "And I'm not a servant. I work my ass off. I'm sorry that you don't see my work as valuable, but I do. Being a child of privilege doesn't mean I don't want to do something with my life. Maybe you fell up into your job but I'm no servant, Darren! I'm not a pet that you get to keep locked up in some house in Arlington Hills popping out babies!"

"I didn't mean it like that, Sanne. Look, I love you. You're not going to say it?"

"Pull the car off at this exit."

"What?"

"I'm taking Metra home," I said. "I'll take the damn train. I want out of this car."

"Baby, what the hell is going on with you?"

I took a deep breath and shouted, "Let me out of the car! Now!"

He weaved through traffic and pulled off at the exit.

"I don't even know where the damn station is," he protested.

"Just let me out. I'll figure it out," I told him.

"No, you won't."

He pulled into a shopping plaza and parked as I cried. "I'm sorry, Sanne. Maybe this wasn't a good time—"

"It wasn't, no," I sobbed. "I just want to get home. That's all."

He took off, driving in silence on surface roads. It took forever but I suspected we both would rather have been moving instead of sitting on the expressway. He drove me to my building. We sat there, his flashers on, for a minute. I couldn't look at Darren. I have been crying for half an hour. My makeup was a mess. I hated myself. I hated everything. I wanted out but I also knew I was about to break his heart. Darren deserved better than this. He wanted to *marry* me. I wanted nothing to do with that. I just couldn't go there. As my sister said, I should not settle.

"You mean a lot to me," I finally looking over at him.

He reached for my hand. "You do, too, Sanne—"

"No," I pulled my hand back, shaking my head and crying. "It's not fair to you for me to just... I don't know what I want. But I do know that I don't love you. I wanted to but I don't. I can't will it. You're a wonderful guy, Darren. You're sweet and respectful and your parents are so normal. I will miss you, but I can't do this anymore."

I hopped out and reached in to get my purse.

Darren stared, an angry expression on his face. "Is there someone else? That Prince? Paul? Is this what this about?"

"No. I fucking hate him," I answered. "I went to impress my clients. I went to not be rude. I just… I can't do this."

I slammed the car door shut and stepped back towards my building's front door, sobbing. The doorman opened the door for me.

"Thanks," I sniffled.

"You alright, Miss Holmes-Nordgren?" he asked.

"Not really. I will be." I called the elevator.

I wondered what the hell I have done. I cried and threw my purse onto the couch. I tossed my throw pillows around and screamed. I just wanted a nice day. I just wanted life to make sense. I just wanted to feel normal. Will I *ever* feel normal? I don't know. I sobbed. I then did the only thing I could think of doing.

"Mamma?" I sobbed into the phone.

"*Hej, min skat,*" she answered.

Mamma called me her *treasure*. It was sweet even if it sounded bad to Americans.

"Are you in the city?" I cried.

"Yes, sweetheart."

"Can I come over and order a pizza?" I squeaked out.

"Oh, sweetheart, what is wrong?" she asked.

"I just broke up with Darren."

"Oh, min skat, I'm sorry."

She's trying to be sweet but also wants to celebrate. I can see it now.

"I don't want to be alone, Mamma."

"Well, come over and Mom and I will order a pizza. She will make you a drink, okay?"

"Sounds lovely," I sniffled.

I packed an overnight bag and hopped on the redline. I was there in no time. I collapsed into my mom's arms. She smelled like Dior. She felt safe. I sobbed. *Why am I so sad?*

"If I didn't love him, why do I care?" I cried.

"You were with him a long time. It was sudden. I think sometimes our feelings can hit hard. It's a lot to manage, I think."

"What's the matter, sweetheart?" Mom asked. "Mamma said you had a fight with Darren."

"I broke it off," I answered.

"Come here, come here." Mom hugged me and kissed my cheek, "Time to drink."

I followed them into the kitchen. Mamma ordered a pizza and Mom made me a mojito with two shots. I was grateful. I explained what happened and they were supportive. They did not do a happy dance or say, "I told you so." They did not make fun of me for being their twenty-eight-year-old daughter crying on their shoulders.

"Well, when you know it's not right, you know," Mom said.

Mamma nodded. "And he said he didn't think you should be working. No, no, no."

"Right? God, I was so angry!"

"So, when he left, did he feel like you let him down gently?"

"He accused me of cheating on him with George's brother. So, no. He thinks I'm a bitch. Which, fair. Like… he's an okay guy. Someone will be lucky to have him. Maybe I wasted his time?"

"Oh, sweetheart, no." Mamma shook her head.

"Is this Prince Paul?" Mom made eye contact with Mamma.

I suspected this has been a topic of conversation around here for a bit.

"Yes," I looked at my drink.

They both stared.

"It's not true. Jesus! I went to a polo match so I didn't offend our clients, Mamma. Stop staring at me like that."

"You didn't give him *any* reason to believe it?" Mamma asked.

"No. I *loathe* him. I call him The Frog. He's literally in my phone as The Frog. I refuse to acknowledge he could be a prince."

"He's in your phone?" Mom asked, ready to tease me.

"Mom, don't go there! Don't be ridiculous. I cannot *stand* him, okay? Not at all."

"Uh-huh," Mamma said before snickering.

"If I were Darren, I'd be paranoid over that," Mom noted. "Because straight men are insecure beasts. I am not saying that he was right. Just… I could see why he would say that."

"He's a pretty boy," Mamma said.

"Mamma, he's not that pretty. Okay, he *is*, but he's insufferable. I couldn't ever bother with him. He's like such a douche. He thinks so highly of himself. He makes these corny-ass jokes. He has no manners. He's not like George at all. Trust me. I can't stand him. I tolerate him—at best."

I meant it. I didn't like Paul. I didn't like him *at all*.

fear and self-loathing in edinburgh

. . .

paul

In late April, George and I landed in Edinburgh for our second-cousin's stag. Gerry was in good spirits, hosting us all at his family's castle in the Scottish borders. I initially looked forward to this weekend—months ago when we planned it, but now the relations of the best man and groom's brother were tenuous-at-best. Even after a "no bad feelings" dinner with the newlyweds, George was prickly about Winston. Lucy and Patrick improved things along with their diplomacy. However, now on his own, George was a loose cannon. Add booze and we were in for a hell of a stag weekend. I would have to babysit when all I wanted to do was get pissed.

For two weeks, things remained calm. George was in good spirits after our last polo match. There, I met his expectations and did not completely embarrass myself. I had not run into Sanne. I wasn't thinking about her as much anymore. Instead, I was focused on chatting up random women at a nearly royal stag.

I wanted it to be like old times where I would go out with the older boys and try to keep up. That ship had long sailed. We were day drinking on Saturday at Mum's family's Scottish tasting room when I realised things changed. It had nothing to do with George's axe to grind, either.

People say marriage changes people. They were not kidding. Winston and Lucy were married for about a month. She took up all the space in Winston's brain. For the life of me, I couldn't understand. As he returned from calling Lucy, Winston looked chipper. He was relieved to hear her voice, I suspected. I saw George's face fall. It was so awkward. I wanted to bail.

"So, you're already on lockdown," said Mark, a friend of Gerry's.

I don't know how Gerry knew Mark. I assumed they went to St. Andrews together.

Winston answered, "Nah. She's in Iceland right now with Natalie. They have some big event later and she's going to go right to bed after the thing is over. She told me she'd call after they landed. I joked that I hoped Natalie didn't kill her on the way up there."

"Nat flew?" George sounded sad.

"Yeah. She flew. Apparently, it was a whole fight."

"Nat never tells me anything anymore," George sighed.

God, is he sad about this? Is he pining for Natalie to talk to him more? Heaven help us!

"Are you all going back to London?" Winston asked. "They'll be back in a couple of days—"

"No. Patrick has matches. We're headed back Stateside on Saturday afternoon."

I joked. "With hangovers."

We could have taken time to visit London. Patrick's mum was visiting and helping with Charlotte. However, George still felt like an outlaw. I knew he felt uneasy sticking around London too long. I felt similarly. Best to keep our noses clean.

"Winston, are you joining us for George's stag?" Nick, Sweden's Crown Prince asks.

Part of our inner circle, his father is a good friend of ours. He went to Eton just like George, Winston, and Gerry.

Winston took a big sip of whisky. "No. I do not think it's a great idea."

"Why?" Nick was already pissed.

"He's probably busy." I don't know if I was trying to save face or what. I wanted anything to stick.

"What? For George's stag? That's stupid!"

"Well, if Winston hadn't fucked my ex-girlfriend, it might be slightly less awkward."

Everyone at the table wanted off the train, except Nick who drunkenly delighted in pushing this button. Winston looked ready to punch George. I would have if someone said that about my wife.

"What? Unpopular opinion?" George grumbled. "Look, I'm sorry. It was low hanging fruit."

"She's my wife, Georgie. My wife. Yes, everyone and their dog knows that you and Lucy were together. Don't we all? Please just respect her–and us."

"Tell me one thing, cousin," George continued.

I cut him off. "No, George. No. We're done with this. Let's just drink and have a good time, alright?"

Winston crossed his arms. "No, no, let him continue to dig his stupid fucking hole."

George set his jaw. "I was about to ask if you all got married in a hurry because of... circumstances."

"Yeah, our dads are dickheads. We told you that."

"I meant... did you knock her up?"

Winston stood, leaning over the table to glare at George. He looked intimidating in a rare case of him trying to throw his weight around. And given that Winston had six inches and probably three stone on George, he could take him. A vein popped out in his neck. Gerry and I scrambled to pull them apart.

"You think it's a fucking joke, don't you? You left her without a place to live or a single idea what she was going to do.

She was in limbo with her visa. If it hadn't been for Gerry and Sheena, she'd have been fucking homeless," Winston said. "She won't ever call you a selfish prick, but I will. You're acting like a child!"

"I'm sorry that me freeing her from settling for a man who wasn't good for her in the end was so bad."

"I didn't say that. I said you did it with no foresight and you didn't think about how it would make her feel. Did she tell you that you gave her a bloody complex for ages?"

"You mean the whole thing about her pussy turning men into stone?" George asked.

"What?"

"Oh-kay," Gerry announced. "And scene. We're done here, gentlemen. I do not need this to come apart at the seams before we even make it through dinner. Alright? So, come on, back on the party bus. Pack in."

We left the tasting room.

I pulled George aside onto the back of the bus. "You cannot talk about Lucy's... body... in public. You're already pissed off your head. If you keep drinking, I will call us a car and turn us right round to come home."

I felt like Mum shouting that she would turn the car around.

"She said that I gave her a complex because she thought it was like some awful reverse-magic. Her pussy isn't a gorgon, full disclosure. It's quite nice. I shouldn't mention that, should I? Shit! It just came out! I regret it now. Fuck, can we just... God. How do I even apologise?"

"You can't and should not. Not now anyway. Give Winston some space. Can you just be good... for once?"

"I don't know," George answered.

We rode along through the fields back to the house, where a full dinner spread was in progress. George kept more to himself at this point. Winston seethed but minded himself for Gerry's sake. It wasn't brilliant. We sat for dinner. George was uncomfortable and decided, in his own great wisdom, to talk to Winston.

"Look, mate, I am sorry. Really."

"Do not make me come for you here, George. I will. It is my family's house. Someday, Lucy will be the lady *of* this house. I am here to try to have fun and to celebrate my brother. Gerry fucking deserves that. And as his best mate, you can understand, right? Don't fuck with me."

Winston was not playing.

"Sure. I thought I was making a joke. It wasn't funny. I'm done. Okay?"

"Just sit down, Georgie," I groaned. "Just sit."

Winston smiled at me a bit while George rounded the table and sits by me, as if giving thanks.

I am sympathetic. I love Lucy. She was the only girlfriend my brother had who I liked. My brother dated a lot of women *until* Lucy. Many treated me like the annoying little brother I was. Lucy, though, was sweet. She was so kind. I couldn't say a bad word about her. Much like our Mum, she was the saintly, dutiful type of girl you couldn't whinge about.

I reasserted the goal again after dinner as we packed to leave for a night of debauchery.

"Behave, George. I swear to God. Do not cockblock me. I haven't gotten laid in *months* and I want to this evening. Can you imagine?"

"No. I don't think I've had more than a five-night dry spell since I was about eighteen," George remarked. "Well, maybe nineteen. How are you surviving?"

"There's this thing called porn. Have you tried it?"

"Jesus. We have got to get you laid. I tell you what, I know I am public enemy number one, but I will try my best to—"

"I can manage to get laid on my own accord, thanks," I assured. The *last* thing I needed was George's "help."

"Cool, cool. Well if you need help—"

I am beyond annoyed with George. I hate when he treats me

like some sort of experiment. You would think he was the only person in the world who managed to have sex. Truth be told, I never struggled with this until recently. Could I have been more aggressive and made it work? Yes, but someone broke my heart. Despite my assertions that the best way to get over someone was to get under them, I wasn't much for a rebound. Having had that–at least in my mind–spoiled me for a cheap one-night stand.

We landed at the first club, exactly the place you would expect. The women were fit enough. Predictably, Gerry and Winston were boring as hell. George was trying not to anger anyone. I tried chatting up a few women, landing on a pretty blonde, Diana, in a teal dress that barely covered her arse. I wondered how she wasn't freezing. Scotland in April was still barely tolerable and certainly no better than Chicago in April. I did not ask her. Some things were best left a mystery.

We ended up snogging like teenagers. Of course, soon as I made out with her, everyone wanted to leave. I had a crucial decision to make. I could either try to convert this thing with Diana into something and hedge my bets on her or I could move along solo and see what other fish there were in the sea. I decided to take Diana with me. She was fun. All I knew was that she had a chihuahua, lived with two other girls, and went to the University of Edinburgh. Which also meant she was too young for me.

Fortunately, she had legs up to her neck, nice enough tits, and didn't seem like a madwoman. It made up for any worries about age. Since I had no security detail, I could go and do as I pleased. Part of me missed the organised, quiet life in the palace walls. All of me hated dealing with PPOs chasing me. For this brief period of my life, I was living like George–a private citizen. Though back in the UK, we both waived detail rights on this trip. I would hook up if it killed me.

Around three or so, while the others headed back to the hotel we'd rented as a crash pad, Diana and I ferried in a cab to her place. We had less-than-mind-blowing-but-sufficient sex and I didn't stay. There was no way that I was going to be like a carnival show for her friends when they woke the next morning. I did not give her my number. I left, arriving back at the hotel as the sun came up. Men were strewn about on any sleeping surface in the suite.

I yanked a pillow from George's bed—lucky bastard—and curled up in the bath. Drunk, post-coital me was happy to sleep anywhere. Overall, the night was a success. Winston had not smashed George to bits, even though he had a right to. Gerry had a brilliant time out with his mates. I had gotten laid for the first time in an eternity. We all survived. No one died and there were no international incidents. We were well-behaved by a stag party's standards. No calls from Dad. We'd be headed back to America soon where the pipe dream of a hook-up would vanish. It seemed impossible as I lived a house with two gay men and their toddler. Ah well, it was good for me.

spa day

* * *

sanne

Every year around Easter, my sister and niece did something called Auntie's Day. They would spoil the hell out of me. I was my sister's ride or die. We shared a womb. That kid was a part of me, too, and I would have killed for her. Because I helped them and made Mother's Day magical every damn year—Jeff doesn't do shit for her like most fathers—I got an Auntie's Day. I never knew when to expect it. On this occasion, Marie handed me a spa gift card for a full day of pampering. Linny scheduled a whiskey tasting to *follow* the spa. It was as if the day were made for me.

More notably, my sister packed *two* pulpy, delightful romance novels to read while I had my salt tub soak and quiet time between treatments. I could pick and choose or spend all day devouring both. I was so pleased and felt loved.

Our parents owned a stake in the hotel with the spa, so Linny and I went there a lot. We could drink standard drinks for free, but I always tipped triple times. The staff were good. The clients were often assholes. Again, FIPs.

The spa manager was Aksel, a gruff bear of a Swede who

took no nonsense from spa goers. He could be downright lovely or a terrifying Viking. My mother spent more money on facials than any human being had a right to spend. She was a regular here. He got me started for the moment with a fluffy robe and sweet cushy slip-ons.

I had my first soak of the day, followed by a massage. It was bliss. I knew I should do it more often. My shoulders bred their own tension. I needed it badly. Ninety minutes passed in a flash. I was relaxing with a refreshing cup of lemon water and my book when I was rudely interrupted. The person I least wanted to see emerged from the changeroom.

"Sanne?"

There was The Prince hovering, also in a robe. *No, no, no!* This was an epic nightmare.

"Sorry, I just had to say hello," he spoke as if we were friends.

His tone was loud. He had no inside voice.

"Uh, hi," I kept my voice down.

"You here for what?"

"Uh, I am here today for a variety of things," I whispered, trying to emphasize the necessary tone of voice.

"Ah, nice."

"You?" I felt obligated to ask.

"Massage. Really fucked up my shoulder last week falling off a horse."

"Ouch," I said, concerned.

I had been there and had some sympathy.

"Figured it couldn't hurt. Are they good? I have someone named Jazz doing my massage. Do you know a Jazz?"

"She's a she." I sensed he looked for the pronoun. "She's fabulous. I have bruises on my shoulder right now but I needed deep tissue."

"Good, good. Yeah, I need a lot of work."

I returned to my book, praying he would move along. I needed Auntie's Day more than ever. Paul here on a fucking Friday in the middle of April was *not* helping me zen. Maybe he would hit on Jazz? Jazz wasn't into men, but he seemed like the type who might at least *try*.

"The romance novel thing. That's hip now?" Paul asked.

"Hip?" I looked up as he settled with a cup of tea.

"Yeah? I guess women aren't ashamed to read that stuff anymore. It's popular now. Even my sisters will do it. You should see Kiersten's collection. She's always looking for a happily-ever-after somewhere."

"I can't blame her. It's nice to read a good book. Why are romances shameful? Is it because they are targeted at women and usually written by women?"

"No, I just... they can be entertaining. But cutesy."

"My life is full of enough drama that I can get behind a happy ending when I find it," I shrugged.

"Well, I mean that's what you do... happy endings, right?" He made a face and looked embarrassed. "I probably shouldn't say that in a spa. I don't want the masseuse to think I would assume that was a *thing*. Foot-in-mouth disorder and all."

"You are a hot mess." I laughed a bit.

It was genuinely funny. He landed one in 1000. I granted that much.

"I am, yeah. So, what are you up to these days? Plans? You hanging around?"

Paul's voice was loud.

Aksel came around the corner and used an accent so thick my mother would sound like a native speaker, "Sir, spa voices. Please keep it down."

"Sorry, sorry," Paul winced.

Aksel asked in Swedish if he was bothering me. I reply in Norwegian that he's fine.

"What is that?" Paul whispers.

"He's Swedish. I'm half-Norwegian. It's just a thing."

"Is that like a... Michigan thing?"

"No," I said, annoyed. "My mother is Norwegian. She knows Aksel. He knows me. It's just a thing we know."

"Oh, oh. Okay."

My esthetician came out and asked quietly but rather auspiciously, "Brows or chin today?"

If I could have died, I would.

"Brows," I replied, face beet red.

It is true that I occasionally wax my chin, as do many women. I am not a particularly hairy person. And, as a fair-skinned human, I puff up like a peach afterwards. So, getting my eyebrows done is problematic enough. Well, at least Paul wouldn't show interest in me anymore.

"Is that *the* prince?" Hazel, the brow miracle worker asked in the treatment room.

"Yeah," I said. "He's a pain in the ass."

"Really? He's hot."

Completely. To the point I sometimes fantasized about him fucking me against a wall. I thought about it too much. I had a dream about it once. The day I last saw him would be the best day of my life. Instead, I didn't give that away. I nodded and confirmed that, yes, Paul was hot. Hazel goes on about things people know about "The Princes" around here. I neither confirm nor deny anything because I've signed an NDA. This wedding is crucial, as is discretion. I merely listen to her exciting guesses about wedding details. Everyone at the hotel has probably signed an NDA if they are working on the wedding. I'd have to ask my mom. She's handling that side of the vendors.

I try to ignore wedding talk. That's business. This is pleasure. Finally, Hazel plucked and pulled my eyebrows into sculpted perfection. I smile. She sends me to the salt whirlpool before my facial, my last treatment of the day. I've asked for my mother's favorite person. My mother is near 60 but looks mid-40s. I hope I inherit that characteristic. I grab my book and head to the whirlpool. It is heavenly up there. However, when I arrive, there is Prince Sexy looking as expected, shirtless, just maxing and relaxing.

"They had a session run over," he said. "I elected to come up here rather than wait 30 minutes."

He sensed that I was in no mood for him.

I nod and sit, using my book as a tiny pink-and purple shield to ignore him.

"Your eyebrows look… lovely. I… I think they are nice."

"Um… okay."

"It was a compliment."

"Okay. But like… was it?" I said, voice flat.

"Yes, it was. You have a lovely face." His voice sounded hurt. "Do you hate me?"

The answer was probably yes.

"No, I don't hate you," I said. "Thanks. I thought you were being mean."

"I'd never take the piss about a face like yours. You have great skin. That's all."

"And how would you know?"

"I dunno. I'm vain. George and I both are. I want to take good care of my skin, alright?"

"I'm not judging you. I'm surprised, but it's not a judgement."

He smiled back and nodded. I thought he was staring at my boobs for a moment. I questioned the intelligence of calling him out for a minute. *Fuck it.*

"Um… are you staring at my chest?"

"Sorry!" He flushed red. "Um… I am trying not to. But there isn't… there is not much to this swimsuit and… you have… you're pretty."

I snickered at his attempt to brush off the fact that he's staring at my breasts while also admitting that he is.

"What? I am sorry but they are… distracting."

"Like a half-naked man in riding breeches that leave little to the imagination wandering into my planning consult?" I asked.

"Fuck, I'm sorry about that, okay? I feel bad about it. I wasn't trying to be a knob, Sanne."

"You weren't trying to parade around and show off?"

"Show off what? I was sweaty and dehydrated. I wasn't trying to put on a show."

I shot him a look that said I didn't buy what he was selling.

"I wasn't."

I scoffed, "Uh-huh. You realise that your body is like... impeccable. Like woah. You know that."

"You defy logic!"

"Are you or are you not hot?"

"I won't confirm or deny that!" I flustered him.

"Look, I say defy logic because I did think you and your sister were your mums. And you weren't. Why on Earth would I attempt to thirst trap two lesbians?"

"See—you admit it! You were thirst-trapping!"

"Sanne, that is *not* a thing! Look, we got off on the wrong foot but... I apologize. I'm not a wanker. I promise you."

Yes, I thought to myself. Yes, we did. And maybe I could have been more generous. At the same time, I found Paul unsettling and annoying.

"What are you doing after this?" Paul asked.

Boy, he is brave!

"I have a facial. And then a tasting scheduled down at the bar. This is a day of rest and relaxation for me—or it should be."

Paul looked contrite. "Oh, shit. I've blown your day up."

"No. But nice try." I laughed it off. At this point, I wasn't sure what I was doing. I wasn't good at being mean. The Prince was awkward, not intentionally rude.

"Look, I don't want us to have bad blood, right? I appreciate the work you do. George adores you. You seem like a nice girl. I wish you no ill will, Sanne."

I nodded.

My facialist appeared. I left the whirlpool, pulled on a towel, and turned, realizing that he was *totally* looking at my ass.

"We're okay," I say. "We'll never be besties, but now that I know you weren't trying to be a complete asshat, I will let it go."

"I was not, no."

As I grabbed my bag, the massage therapist arrived for Paul. He emerged from the whirlpool like the sexy hero from a corny rom-com. I attempted not to stare.

How in the hell is he so hot? How? I hate him. I still fucking hate him. I will just pretend to hate him less now. I still hate him, though.

your worst nightmare

. . .

paul

"Can I bother you, Jazz? What is this about a whiskey tasting?"

I just finished a lovely massage but spent the entire time thinking about every bit of Sanne, and her mention of the whiskey tasting.

"It's bourbon, not your type of whiskey, I'm afraid," she explained.

"Oh, well, my mother is a bourbon heiress, so... I love all kinds."

"Oh, really? Well, cool. It's across the way in the restaurant. You buy a ticket and get a tasting and dinner with parings. We do it a few times a year. I can call over and see if they have a space open if you'd like?"

"That would be lovely, thanks," I answered.

"Okay. Well, you get dressed and I'll meet you at the desk."

I stopped in the doorway. "Oh, one more thing. Well two. One, what is the dress code? Two, if you *can* get a ticket and it's casual, can they seat me by Sanne?"

Jazz gave a sly smile. "Dress code here is always casual and I will see what I can do. You like her?"

I shrugged. "I sort of am trying to make her not hate me. I have a plan."

"I don't think she hates you!"

"I think she does. She says she doesn't. Her face shows only derision."

"I will do my best, okay? Chin up." Jazz winked.

I leave, shower, and dressed, meeting Jazz to settle the bill.

"So, you are set. Dinner starts in 45 minutes but feel free to get a drink before. Also, I was able to get them to squeeze you in near Sanne," Jazz said.

"Thank you," I left her a massive tip.

I still wasn't sure what I was doing. As I left, I realised I orchestrated this without a plan. She would know I decided to attend the whiskey tasting because she said she was. I've already made her want to punch me for disturbing her peace. However, I knew I *could* be charming when I wanted. The issue is that I didn't know how to woo her. More importantly, I was not sure *why* I was wooing her. Yes, I found her attractive. She acted like she knew I did. That was a good sign. Hopefully, she didn't just abhor me.

The thing with Sanne was that the more I was around her, the more I wanted her to like me. I suppose I'm a people pleaser. That is the difference between me and my twin older siblings. I need to be loved. I take after my mother. Everyone loves my mother because she's so charming and affable, but I'm as awkward as my father. Sanne not liking me was difficult to stomach. I didn't think she was the centre of the universe. I swear I didn't. I just always need everyone to love me. As I had recently been a pariah, this seemed especially pressing.

I sat at the restaurant bar. It was nice enough. The bartender, some short, peppy guy named Layton, kindly showed me the cocktail list. He treated me like a normie. I always worry that in these cases, someone is going to see me and be over-the-top. Being overrun with royal watchers is awful. I worried about that, but my biggest worry was upsetting Sanne. She arrived fifteen minutes later and bellied up to the bar to order her own drink. The look on her face was between pure hatred and mild annoyance. I couldn't tell with Sanne yet. I had spent almost two months around but still barely knew her.

"Put hers on my tab," I said.

Sanne protested. "You really don't have to do that."

"I'm not arguing with you. I owe you. I am trying, Sanne."

Sanne rolled her eyes and let out the most annoyed "thanks" ever uttered. Somehow, I found this encouraging. The more she dug in, the more I wanted her.

"Lemme guess what you're doing," she said as a Sazerac arrived.

"Go on."

"I bet you're about to crash my dinner."

"And why would you guess that?"

"Because you are fucking predictable."

"I am *not* predictable."

She burst into a fit of laughter. "You are a hero straight out of a Hallmark Channel original. You're terrible."

"I don't get that reference. Is that a compliment?"

"It's not a compliment, Paul. No. Well, I guess it depends. They are sappy romance movies. Think men who just pop up in a cozy little Christmas village and sweep the work-obsessed female lead off her feet. In your case, a prince who finds a future princess working at a butcher shop or something. In the end, they either move to Vermont to run a restaurant or open a bakery together that makes only Christmas cookies."

"That's something my sister would glom onto like anything. Coming from a woman who reads romance novels, should you really cast stones?"

"Look, I'm not here to yuck your sister's yum. I'm sure she's lovely. It's not for me. My stories never end with a woman giving up her career to move to fucking New England. And I don't read stories about royals."

I shrugged. "They're probably inaccurate. So, do you bake pies, Sanne?"

She rolled her eyes and drank her saz. "You're making my point. You're a walking dad joke, Paul."

"Is there anything wrong with that? So, I'm not cool. I never claimed to be, darling."

"So, do you advocate moving to Vermont to turkeys? Do *you* bake cookies? What is your plan?"

"I wouldn't plan to move to Vermont. I think I must go back eventually. I have no plan. More than likely, I will go help my sister. I don't know. I'm trying to figure my fucking life out right now, honestly."

"But does the heroine in your silly royal romance drop everything to pop out heirs or whatever it is she's supposed to do? How does your sappy story end, Paul?"

I was slightly annoyed. Did she think my life was a joke?

"Oof, you think so highly of us, Sanne."

The thing is, I knew I could give it back as good as I gave it. I found her charming.

She twirled the stir stick in her glass. "I asked you a question. What happens to your poor princess? Royal wedding? Twenty babies? She should be meek and willing, yeah?"

"I don't like to think about it like that. Nor would I ever class my dear mother that way. She's a brilliant human being. My father would fall to bits without her. If anything, the men in my family don't deserve the women who keep it running—that includes those who support my mother and sister. It's far more complicated than showing up and cutting ribbons. Maybe it's silly, but it's a lot of emotional labour. In my mum's case, it was the physical labour that went into having and raising four kids."

"You want four kids?"

"Sanne, you are so quick to make assumptions."

"Like you were when you invited me out to impress me at that polo thing? But then didn't ask me if I had a boyfriend?"

I blushed. I tried not to, but she had gotten me there. She had seen right through me.

"I… uh… I may have unintentionally invited you assuming that."

"You literally gave me your number, Paul!"

"But why did you come? Did you actually want to come?"

"I didn't want to offend your brother and Pat."

"Likely answer. Why bring the boyfriend? I didn't suggest you bring him—no one did. If I invited you again, would you bring him?"

She looked cross. "We broke up."

"He dumped you?"

"Excuse me! Now *you* are making assumptions. I've never been dumped!"

Shit. I'd gotten myself into a bit of a pickle.

"Why are you such an absolute dickhead?" she asked. "You actively treat women like shit—"

"Just you. And it's not intentional," I admitted.

"Why then?"

"You make me nervous, and I trip over myself."

She sat there, realising I'd admitted I liked her. I didn't know what more to say.

Thankfully, her tempered voice chimed. "I dumped him. He wanted me to stay home and have babies while he made money and 'took care' of me."

"Ah, your comments make more sense."

"Yours don't."

"Sanne, I am sorry for acting like a nervous dickhead around you. I invited you out to the polo so I could impress you some-how. I don't know why… I really don't know why."

"Why do you even care? I haven't given you any reason to believe I like you!"

"Because every time I chat with you, I realise you're brilliant. You have your shit together. Perhaps, I just admire that in you? Perhaps, I'm jealous I don't have my own shit together? All I know is I am attracted to you. You make my palms sweat and my pulse race. I become an inarticulate goon around you. I hate it. It's unintentional, though."

"You think I have my shit together?" Sanne let out a laugh. "That is cute."

"Well, you manage the business stuff well. You are authoritative. It's as unsettling as it sexy, Sanne."

She looked at me, mouth gaping. A man announced the tasting was about to begin. I prayed I got what I asked for. Sanne silently downed her drink.

"We should—"

"Head over, yeah," Sanne agreed, finishing my thought.

We reached our table. We were seated across from one another. There was a lecture about the process and the menu. Sanne busied herself on her phone. All I could think about was how badly I had just bombed it all. Moreover, I felt this primal urge to kiss her. I thought for sure that would fix it all. I would make it clear I wanted her at that point.

Sanne looked up from her phone as our first course arrived. "It's fine."

"What is? Sorry." Her statement confused me.

She tossed her hair over her shoulder. "That you like me, I guess."

"Oh, I'm *allowed* to fancy you. Alright, thanks for the permission."

"Are you going to make fun of me or what?"

"That was me flirting with you, actually."

"Glad you explained it."

"Perhaps, it's getting lost in translation that I am trying to get into your knickers but I am."

It was a possibly-mortifying bout of verbal diarrhoea. *Fuck! Cocked that up.*

She took a deep breath, her brow furrowed. The wheels were turning. She took a massive swig of whisky and set her glass down definitively.

"You will have to try *much* harder if that is your goal."

I wanted to kiss her even more. It was the first indication I had she was *flirting* with me. My excitement must have been palpable at that moment, as she did this cute thing where she bit her lip and tucked her hair behind her ear. I had an immediate urge to kiss her neck. I wanted to devour her.

"The gauntlet has been thrown?" I tried playing cool.

"How you interpret it is up to you, Paul."

"Well, I must try harder, I suppose."

"You really think you can improve your chances that much?" Sanne asked.

"I know I can."

"That's cute. I am not sure there is anything you can do."

"Well, I'm game to try."

"Do women ever turn you down?" Sanne asked.

"Not often, no. Sometimes, even I can't manage it."

"What do you mean?"

"Someone just shattered my heart into pieces. Even I can get dumped, Sanne."

That vulnerability somehow smoothed things over.

Her face softened. "I get it. I mean, I don't get dumped but I get that the end of a relationship just sucks. What makes you think you can pull this out?"

"Because you already admitted you think I'm hot," I chuckled. "I think we'd be great together."

"Wanting to have sex with you is not the same as enjoying your company generally."

That only made me want her more.

"Okay, well, I'll take what I can get and hope maybe I could convert you. What are you up to after this?"

"You cannot be serious!"

"I asked a question, Sanne."

Sanne blushed. "I am staying with my sister and can't go back there. I suspected the same for you with your family."

"We'll make it work," I assured.

no tell motel

· · ·

sanne

I sat at the bar. Paul and I flirted *heavily* through dinner, and I wasn't sure what to think. Had he indicated a willingness to fuck me even though I wasn't sure I even liked him enough to bother. Somehow, the cockiness was hot. Don't get me wrong, I still *hated* him. He was terrible. I was just sure of it. I was also convinced there was zero chance we would hook up. And more than that, if we did, there was no way the sex would be good, right?

Then, things got stranger. Paul left while I was in the bathroom. I figured he was an asshole who had just ghosted me but the bartender handed me another drink and said "prince boy" told him to tell me no worries that he would be back. I was miffed. I thought about making eyes at some guy down the bar just to piss Paul off. What on Earth would make sense here that you would leave a girl you were trying to sleep with alone at a bar? It was stupid.

After a bit, Paul returned, looking no different. I had no idea what he had done. He had a small bag in his hand. I was steadily more confused.

"What the hell is going on?" I asked. "What is wrong with you?"

"Forgive me, please. I dipped home."

What?

"You dipped home?"

"Just up the bloody street. To Georgie's."

"Uh-huh."

He sat the bag on the bar. "Finish up there, Sanne."

"What are you doing?" I asked.

Paul fumbled through his pocket. He pulled out a room key and answered me, voice low, "Take this. I'm going to escape. Meet me upstairs in ten."

He rented a room? What *was* this? Part of me was angry. Part of me was impressed. I wanted to shout at him for being presumptuous, but the power move made me want to climb him like a tree. *Well done, Frog.* At this point, it might have been the whiskey talking.

"Are you telling me or asking me?" I asked.

Paul answered, voice assured, "Telling you because I know you'll come. Also, I have edibles."

I snickered. "You think you're hot shit? They're legal."

"Look, do you want to fool around or not? You threw down the gauntlet, not me."

Touché.

Fine," I agreed, annoyed with him.

"I like it when you're cross with me. Makes me fancy you more," Paul departed.

He was downright smarmy. I hated that. I also wanted to make him suffer. Perhaps, I could put his desire to woo me to good use?

I held the key card in my hand. I could either ghost *him* or go along with a bit of fun. If I turned him down, I would be a gigantic bitch, but would show him was the condescending asshole I still very much believed he was. If I ended up going for it, it could be fun. I would at least *know*, right? And what if it was really good hate sex? Hate sex was a thing, right? Maybe it was worth the chance. If I left, I was going to blow things up. If I stayed, things might be interesting. The choice was clear. I texted Linny to tell her I would be out late and not to stay up. I slammed the rest of my drink.

"He settled the bill. You're good," Layton said. "He's a generous tipper, if it matters."

It was like he said it to encourage what I was stupidly about to do. Even Layton could sense I wasn't sold on this. He didn't know me *that* well, but like any local I'd drank at this bar enough. We all knew one another. And now everyone in Buffalo Shores could guess what we were up to. I nodded and departed, taking the elevator to the top floor. I entered the room, not sure what the hell I would find. I found Paul drinking a coke and having a small bit of the cookie.

"You made it?" Paul tried not to look surprised.

He was nervous.

"I did."

"Have trouble finding it?"

"God, no. This is pretentious, you know?"

"What is?"

"Booking the bridal suite for a hook-up."

I rolled my eyes and bit the cookie. "Don't go too hard on that. Have you ever done edibles before? It's best to take a bite and wait."

"I have, thank you very much. I'm not that much of a page boy. Also, how did you—"

"I cannot count the number of times I have gotten this room ready either for a bride to *get* ready or to set it up for other people to fuck in that bed in there. In fact, it makes me a bit queasy."

"Get over yourself. I have fucked in beds that were hundreds of years old and it's fine," Paul assured. "Every one of our houses is loaded with ghosts, I'm certain. Best not to think of it."

I snickered. "Did you eat the edible before you came back?"

"Yep. It's hitting about now."

"Fair. I've also been feeling a bit of a buzz since they used CBD and THC in my facial. My mom swears by it. I didn't mention it. It is probably clouding my judgement," I said.

"I'm okay with cloudy judgement."

"Me, too, ironically."

I sat by him on the couch.

He said, "I also had to run home for condoms, which I also... well they aren't necessarily going to—"

"You didn't need to tell me that but it's good you did... run home. Because I didn't have any. I brought my gym bag and not my purse. So, none in there."

"You don't bring johnnies to the gym?" Paul joked.

"Nope. Not sure I like the idea of sweating profusely and then having sex."

Despite saying that, I admitted that I really did appreciate Paul half-naked and sweaty. Despite my attempts to remove that image, it now lived rent free—especially after the whirlpool. I hated him for it.

"I don't know. Could be hot in a pinch?"

I shrugged. "Did you buy the edibles on your little walk or—"

"Nah. I bought them earlier because my shoulder is fucked up. It's better after the massage, thankfully. Jazz is a miracle worker, like you said. I also had a hankering to get stoned and watch a movie. If I was going to be bored anyway, why not?"

"Would you rather be bored or—"

"Nah. I'd rather see you naked," Paul admitted in a way that made me want to tear his clothes off.

I let him kiss me. The feeling of Paul's lips on mine wasn't totally repulsive. It was awkward at first, like any beginning to a make out session with someone you hardly know. However, the way he wound me up is impressive. Paul ran his fingers through my hair, holding it tightly, almost possessively. It was a turn on I didn't know I had.

We kissed for what seemed like ages. Normally, I would have moved things along, but he was having the best time. And, in turn, I was happy to keep kissing him. Eventually, Paul kissed my neck and pulled my dress down to reveal my bra. I didn't stop him. In fact, I wanted him to take my dress off. I pulled his face back up to mine and kissed him hard. Finally, I tossed my dress aside.

Paul took this as a big green light. He undid my bra. I stop him.

I pushed him off. "Look, if you're going to do that, I want you to get naked."

"Go to the bedroom and I promise you I will," Paul said.

I didn't know why I listened to him. I didn't know why he listened to me. We didn't care for one another in a *genuine* sense. Still, we both wanted the same thing.

I rushed into the bedroom, feeling the edible hitting me, and climbed in bed. I left my panties on in what I felt was an act of protest. He slowly and artfully got naked. Paul was the sexiest man I had ever seen in the buff. He was sculpted like a piece of art. was even better nude than half naked. He was also hung. There were no complaints now. I felt no pain and no shame.

"You get to leave your knickers on but you make me strip?" Paul asked.

"You should work a bit."

Paul kissed first between my breasts. He sucked on my right nipple, then my left. It was gentle. Paul didn't respond to my comment.

Perhaps, he likes to be told what to do?

Paul slowly ran his hand down to my panties, flirting with the lace on top. By now, I was very wet. I was ready to beg him to touch my pussy. The logical side of my brain that should have shut this down left. I was left with my lizard brain. It told me to go forth and have a good time. Paul pulled my panties aside, slipping two fingers inside of me. I gasped involuntarily. I had been fantasizing about this. Now, it was real.

"You're wet," Paul said. "Am I at least earning good marks so far?"

"Yeah, well. You're earning excellent *grades*." I correct his Britishism.

Paul silently locked eyes with me and parted my legs. I fully expected him to just go for it. Instead, he pulled my panties off, tossed them aside like he threw them off a stage triumphantly to a crowd of adoring fans, and began to go down on me.

I didn't mind men going down on me. Some had been very good to-date, but most had no idea what they were doing. They'd kill time a bit half-heartedly, demand I blow them, and then get to the "main event." If I even baulked, suggesting that they should have gotten me off, I was considered ungrateful. They would say "I tried" or some such shit. I expected the same from Paul. I almost told him not to bother. I wanted to fuck him and wasn't in the mood for learned helplessness. Plus, one night stands never led to impressive oral sex.

I fought the urge to interrupt. One, because it was hot to watch Paul go to town. He was in true pursuit of my affections. If this was his goodwill campaign, I was okay with it. Paul was fabulous. He used his mouth *and* fingers in a way no one had ever done. He sucked on my clit while stroking my g-spot. It had taken him no time to find either of those willing and waiting. I wanted to believe he was bad at this. It would have been so satisfying. Instead, I found myself ten seconds away from the face of God.

I pulled Paul's hair hard, gripped the comforter with the other hand, and let out a loud moan. My toes curled, my legs twitched, every bit of me felt tingly. For me, edibles made for intense orgasms, but this was other worldly. I realised then what had happened, and I began to panic. It was nowhere near the first time I had squirted but it was the first time I had done so in this way. I wasn't sure if I should address it. Had he noticed? God, I hoped not!

Not only was I afraid I had offended him now, I was also not about to let him feel so satisfied or to let on that this just didn't *happen*.

"Did you just? Do you always—"

"Yes and no," I answered. To my relief, he wasn't offended. To my horror, he patted himself on the back. A stupid grin washed over his face as he pinned me to the bed.

"Don't get too excited. I'm easy to get off. *That* doesn't happen often, but it does happen and, generally, the wind could blow and I could cum."

"Uh-huh." Paul didn't believe me.

He kissed my neck and sent me reeling again. I gasped.

I wrapped my legs around him as he slid inside me. It was legendary level sex. I hated it. Because, after all, I was engaged in hate sex, right?

"Alright?" he clarified. God, he *cared* about me.

"Yeah," I murmured like an idiot. "The pot is hitting good now."

"Sure, that's all," Paul laughed.

I want so badly to ignore him. I also want to believe this is terrible. It isn't, though.

"You want to cum again?"

"I want you to fuck me."

"And why should I let you cum, Sanne?"

"Please, God, let me cum," I begged. He wanted me to beg, and I was doing it. Who the fuck was I?

Paul thrust and pinned my legs back in a way that made me want to die—in a good way. He was gorgeous and intent on pleasing me. I came again, feeling like melting butter. I didn't understand why it even felt like that. He smiled. Oh, he was so satisfied with himself!

"You get on top," Paul said.

"Why, so I can do all the work?"

"No, so I can see your tits bounce around. Is it not fair after me making you completely lose your mind? I want a good view. I want to see you cum again."

"That is unlikely."

He lay down on his back, his abs just screaming for attention. "You said if the wind blew—"

"Fine, we'll see."

I climbed astride and dug my nails into his pecks. God, they were perfect. Being on top was always better, so this was preferable. I had fun tracing the lines on his chest. I didn't know if it was looking that made me lose it or feeling him. It might have been both. It took a moment, but once I put my effort in, I came. It was like seeing fireworks. I was convinced the pot caused my euphoria.

"Yeah, you owe me an apology, darling."

Paul flipped me onto my back in a way that boggled my mind. I was super stoned and feeling useless. He was potentially more stoned and doing acrobatics. How does this work?

Paul went for broke. I was like a puddle lying there, looking up, happy to watch. Every bit of me tingled. I hadn't had three in a row like that in so long I didn't remember. Darren hadn't been *bad* at sex. We'd just been busy and in a rut. Hate sex was different. That is what made this so good.

Paul finally came, slumping over. He gave me a long kiss that I should have probably refused, but I couldn't help myself. I happily lay there with our lips and tongues pressed together with him still inside me. After more kissing, Paul rolled off the bed to deal with the immediate aftermath and I lay there wondering what the fuck we just did.

conversion

. . .

paul

I lay in bed by Sanne, stoned and satisfied. I turned. She stared at the ceiling. Her chest heaved. She was a sweaty mess. Her hair was a disaster. I liked it more than ever. I couldn't tell if she hated me or not. She didn't hate what I did to her. Sanne was, as expected, beautiful. Her skin was like porcelain and the slightly ginger colour of her hair only added to it. She had freckles all over. I'd enjoyed making their acquaintance as I went.

Sanne turned to me, still silent. I reached over and kissed her again. She was a lovely kisser. She had full lips. She was warm. Her skin was terribly soft, and her hair was like silk. I could have played with it all day. The cannabis made this feel much bigger than it was. It gave me the courage to make a move. I couldn't complain. Compared to the girl in Edinburgh, this was like fire. Sanne didn't just scratch an urge. I wanted to devour her now—again and again. Listening to her cumming was music to my ears. She was wonderful.

"You aren't bad at that," she said.

That was the best I was going to get.

"I will work to get good or even exceptional. What mark would you give me?" I asked.

"No fucking comment."

"I will take that as an A. An A+ would be better," I sighed.

"Don't get too cocky."

"You screamed my name the last time you came. No one does that unless they are really enjoying themselves."

"Did I?" Sanne looked mortified.

"Yeah, you did. I loved it."

Sanne rolled her eyes in protest as I flipped on my side.

"What now?" I asked.

"You need to get dressed or I'm going to be tempted to do that again—"

"Give me fifteen and I'm game."

I played with her left nipple. It was so lovely and pink.

She slapped my hand, "No!"

Her tone was forceful. I couldn't tell if she is serious, or this was play. I backed off.

Sanne softened. "I mean… I'm all over the place right now. Maybe I will want to go again. I don't know."

I playfully ran my teeth over her collarbone and kissed her neck. She pretended like she didn't like it. She did. She was playing coy now. That seemed to be her thing.

"So," I asked, "after we go for round two, what then?"

"I have to go home and you should, too. I don't need anyone thinking this is sus, okay?"

"Uh-huh."

"I'm serious. I shouldn't have even done this, Paul. I don't fuck my clients."

"I'm not your client. And look, even if we never do this again, it will not matter, okay?"

"Oh, really?" She didn't believe me.

"George already knows I fancy you. He thinks I'm going to cock it up. He literally does not care if I shag you. He's not going to say boo or hold it against you. Given that he not only fucked but carried on a full-blown relationship with a member of Mum's staff for five years, he's living in a glass house."

Sanne burst into an adorable giggle and touched my face.

"God, that's funny. He really does live in a glass house."

She was stoned. I wanted her all the same.

"He does, yeah. My point is that he's just... George. He doesn't care, alright?"

"My Mom thinks we're going to end up sleeping together. She has practically encouraged it. She thinks I protest too much. As does my sister."

"Uh-huh," I played with her hair absentmindedly.

"Leave it. It's a mess."

"All of you is a mess. I rather like it."

"I hate you," Sanne protested. "I do. That was hate sex."

"You seemed to really *love* it. You find me charming."

"In a way that makes me loathe myself."

"Uh-huh." I didn't buy it.

I ground her gears. We'd do this again. This would preoccupy us both. I had no regrets.

"I suppose we should go after this," I admitted. "I honestly do not want to talk about feelings and shit with George. He's still irritated about something that happened with Gerry's planning of the stupid stag party. I want to remedy it but... he's lousy at it."

"You want to explain to the class what you mean?"

"I'll talk to you about it tomorrow. I might need your help. For tonight, I just want to fuck you again."

I pressed her back against the bed. We went a second round. It was thrilling. I knew her a little better than last time, so I did even better. I could tell that Sanne wasn't much of a cuddler. That was a shame because I was a damn good one, or so people said. We went our separate ways. I dropped my keys at the desk, almost wanting people to know that, yes, I just fucked her, and I was spectacular at it. I resisted the urge to gloat.

I returned, finding George and Patrick in the living room

talking about something related to their honeymoon. I tried to sneak to my room but they were on to me.

"Excuse me," George said. "You're just going to slink away? After whatever it was that brought you back here. You left before I could even ask you what you were on about."

"I'm good. Tired. Going to bed."

"How is your shoulder?" Patrick asked.

"Much better, thanks. Jazz was the one who worked on me. She is ace."

"And?" George asks. "Wait… are you stoned?"

I shrugged. "I'm a little baked."

Patrick snicked. "Sure."

"Look, I'm a lot baked. It is good for my muscles, I think. It's legal. Don't judge me."

"You look all flushed and happy. Did you sleep with someone?" George continued his interrogation.

God, he sounds like Dad.

Because I was stoned, I burst into a fit of laughter.

"What?" George asked, annoyed.

"You sound like Dad. It's so funny."

"You are so stoned," Patrick laughed.

"Yeah, well, I did get laid. It was a triumph. Sorry, not sorry, boys."

I flopped into a chair.

"And?" George asked.

"What, you want a play-by-play? No. We're not doing this. Why, so you can make fun of me? It was great. Full stop. Brilliant."

"Don't pat yourself on the back too hard," Patrick said. "Who is she? Did you just run into her?"

"I did run into her," I lied.

I could tell by George's face he'd ask two dozen more questions.

Because I am weak, I blurt, "It's Sanne. I fucked Sanne. She's amazing. Fuck. Why did I tell you that?"

"Because you have never been able to stop talking," George groaned.

"You can't fuck the planner, Paul!"

"I know, Pat, I know. But she… she makes me so frustrated and then I think about her tits and… God, she's stunning. And fun. And her loathing of me only makes me want her more."

"Paul, you cannot shag our planner!"

"Yeah, you shagged the help—"

"Shut it," George silenced me. "Look, she's a nice girl. Way too smart for you. I have no idea why she would bother but… well done."

"Maybe she will be a force for good? Paul, you could use someone organised and capable in your life."

"Are you saying I am not?" George asked, offended.

"Baby, you are a hot mess express. I love you to pieces. You are my favourite person, but you are a gorgeous disaster. It is what I love about you. I feel useful," Patrick said with a shrug.

I smiled a bit. They were sweet. I liked this for George. He needs it. Patrick is honest and patient, just like my brother prefers. Honestly, I can see the benefit in it. George and I have that in common. George leaned over and kissed Patrick.

"I love you and I hate you," George muttered.

"Yes, I know."

"Maybe that is good. Maybe you will learn from Sanne," George admitted.

"I dunno. What I *do* know is that she's abject perfection, sex on two legs, and I'm going to have her again," I announced.

"Those are high praise, bruv."

"There are some things I cannot explain. Sanne drives me mad. I enjoy her verbal trouncing of me. I always say something wrong. She will take it out on me. However, I know *how* she takes it out on me and I'm game."

"You're the worst," Patrick said. "Both of you. God, why do women bother with that?"

"Powerful, ambitious women like to lose control," George

said. "I always found it tedious to play that game. It wasn't for me. I also like to give up control a bit. But they find it alluring and a bit bad, I think."

"I find this so odd. The idea you would have ever been that way." Patrick shook his head.

"Does it ever bother you?" I asked Patrick.

"No," Patrick answered. "Not really. Unless he becomes an ogre who embarrasses himself over poor Lucy Chandler."

"Now, she's the Countess of Lauderdale," I reminded Patrick. George pulled a face.

"Nah," Patrick said. "No, it doesn't bother me. It's fascinating. For the period of time we were not together, he was in a couple legitimate relationships with women. And, to my knowledge, they weren't all bad. Meanwhile, I was trying to force myself to stay in the closet and forming an alliance with a trying woman. The only reason I don't regret it is Charlotte. Still, I hate having sex with women. It's torturous. I've always just *wanted* to like it—even once. I can't."

"No comment," George muttered.

"It's okay to admit that you still find women attractive, George. *You're* the one with the hang up—not me," Patrick said.

"You're not insecure at all?" I asked.

"Not at all. He left a sure thing—the best choice he *could* have made—to blow up his life and run off with me. It was stupid. I love that George is so brave. I love that he loved me enough to try. I am forever grateful. But, nah. I'm not bothered by it any more than I worry about him running off with anyone."

"Gays aren't... they aren't as possessive as straight people," George clarified. "I still think about things like a straight man *most* of the time—well that shit. It's emblazoned in me, I suppose. Hence, the ogre in me."

"It's sweet you can feel that way," I said. "I guess I've never felt that secure in a relationship. It has led to fighting."

"Is that why you ended things with Katrine?"

"Katrine dumped me. That had something to do with it, yes," I replied.

"He doesn't want to talk about it, Georgie," Patrick said. "Leave him be."

"Okay, fine," George said. "I love you, brother. Very much. I want you to find happiness. However, be *gentle* with Sanne. She is important to us. She's also the daughter of a dear friend. Her mums won't take kindly to you treating her like rubbish."

"Understood. I will be well-behaved," I promised him.

I have no intention of behaving myself.

don't panic

. . .

sanne

I returned to my sister's house, climbing into the guest room bed. I stared at the ceiling, still stoned. The house was silent. It rained. I heard the water coming off the roof. I was strangely at peace despite the tumultuous evening. I expected to be embarrassed by myself. However, that didn't happen. Instead, I felt serene. Part of that was the drugs but part was the feeling of being cared for. Had Paul not *worshipped* my body just now? I didn't even know that was possible.

I fell asleep. I must have been grinning stupidly. When I woke, my niece stood over me like something out of The Shining. She held my phone.

"Who is The Frog? Why is he sayin'… ro-und… round three… and question mark?"

"Hand that to me. It's impolite to read text messages," I said.

She glared.

"You're too smart. Go on, leave me be," I said. "I'll take you to run around if you give me a moment to shower and get put together."

I hopped in the shower, all smiles. Yeah, he's still hung up on me. He can't get enough. I let my hair air dry. I will pull it back before I leave the house and head to my evening event. It's a low-key evening wedding at the same hotel where Paul and I just devolved completely. Still, I kept it together. Paul hasn't got the better of me.

"Good morning, buttercup," Linny laughed as I entered the kitchen. It was a disaster. The countertops were missing from her cabinets. She operated mostly on plywood.

"Stop."

"So, what kept you?" Linny raised her eyebrows, annoyed with me for not giving her a full scoop.

I looked at Marie and lied. "I stayed out."

"Who is The Frog? Is it a fairy-tale thing? You kiss him and he turns into a prince?" Marie asked.

"Yes, and you shouldn't go through people's phones. He's just a guy. I called him a silly name."

Linny looked like she was about to spring into a dozen questions. She was limited by the little pitcher in the room.

"Uh-huh. And he had nothing to do with this?"

"He was there. I can confirm. He showed up for a massage and then tortured me, crashed the dinner, and all that."

"But what happened after?"

"Fireworks. But I still hate him."

"Fireworks?! I missed fireworks!?" Marie had FOMO.

"No, no, Marie. No fireworks. Not *actual* fireworks."

"You are gonna drive me to Indiana so we can buy fireworks! At Fourth of July! They have the good ones!"

"Yes, Marie. Fourth of July."

"I need all the details later. Was it a big load of fireworks or... small? Not that small is bad but..." Linny's voice trailed.

"No, the fireworks were surprisingly big. They did the job." I answered.

My phone began to ring.

"It's Susie," I groaned.

Susie met the vendors for set up. The dinner was at 7. I wasn't due to arrive until 5. It was only 1.

"Hello, Susie?"

"Hey. So, we've got an issue. The caterer called. They are not going to make it."

"It's a *dinner*. The caterer must make it," I said.

I told the couple not to go with this unknown caterer for this reason, but they underbid everyone. Dad, the guy paying, was cheap.

"Yeah, so they didn't have the money to pay the order at Gordon's and now Gordon's won't cover their credit account. So, they didn't buy the food and—"

"Shit," I said.

Linny shot me a look and mouthed, "Language".

I took my phone across the plank and onto the porch, plopping on an old camping chair.

"I'm so angry, I could spit. Barney says they had pot roast on special for dinner service and he would cut us a deal. If we want to do that, he'll give it to us at cost plus ten percent."

"Fine! Do it. Put it on the card," I said. "These are friends of Mom's."

"I know."

"So, how badly do we need chicken and veggie options?" I groaned.

"Badly. The bride doesn't eat meat and the mother of the groom doesn't eat beef."

"Of course. Does the bride know it's a mess?"

"Her idiot brother told her so now we are so fucked."

"Okay, as soon as I can get some pants on, I will be over there," I rushed back across the plank and into the kitchen. "I gotta go. We've got an emergency. Can I steal the van?"

"The van is in St. Joe with Jeff," Linny said.

"Fuck. Fuck. Sorry, Marie… don't repeat what I said."

"But you were going to take me to the beach!"

"I'm sorry. I have a bride having a meltdown, it's a client of

Mormor's, and I have a caterer who isn't going to show. I think I have a plan. I need a larger vehicle. I will figure that out in a minute."

I put on clothing and raced to the venue. The tables looked lovely with elegant linens. The couple couldn't afford Linny. At least the vendor they went with didn't fuck us.

"So, in order of preference we have 30 beef, 100 chicken, and 50 vegetarian," Susie said.

"I have a plan, don't panic," I said.

She beamed at me. *Good, I'm glad Susie believes me!*

I greeted the bride. She was in the suite that Paul and I left the night before. I decided *not* to tell her what we did on top of that bedspread and try not to think about the man I am obviously thinking about. The bride was a pretty and stout woman of about thirty. She looked amazing but was very upset. I talked her down, told her she is lovely—she is—and that everything will be alright. Her father paced in the hallway as persona non-grata. I felt for him. I knew he *meant* well.

"Sanne, we're up shit creek," he said.

"Don't panic," I repeated. "I have a plan. Do you know anyone with a large SUV or pickup?"

"No," he said. "Other than the limo. But that's for the church."

"I got it," I answered. "Um… okay. I will deal with it. The bride is fine. She looks beautiful. We will make this an amazing evening and you'll all have a funny story to tell later."

"I'm going to sue that asshole!"

"And you should," I said. "But right now, it's the bride's day."

I called the only person I know who was nearby and owned a large car.

"Hey, so round 3? I have ideas—"

"Paul, can you be a grownup for two minutes?"

"Does it lead to me having sex with you?"

"I will hang up this phone—"

"What do you need?" Paul asked.

"I will have sex with you. You need to bail me out of a jam, though."

"Okay, I'm listening."

I rolled my eyes, "Can you come with me to Costco?"

"What is a Costco?"

"It's a warehouse store. Fancy a trip to civilization? It's an hour both directions, and we are in a hurry."

"I fancy many things with you in all directions," Paul said.

I wanted to punch his face.

"So will you help me?"

"Yes, darling. Of course."

I rolled my eyes, "Drive over here and bring your car—the big one. I'm at the hotel. Just pull into the valet line. I'll meet you."

"I will bring the big one."

"Stop it! Bring the G."

"I will bring the G."

"Stop saying it like that!"

"You have two more hours of this, darling. Get used to it."

Paul hung up. I hated that he called me darling. I also loved that he called me darling. I wanted to fuck him and kill him. I was a ball of contradictions. I raced downstairs and called on a friend in the area who was a personal chef. I offered to pay her twice her hourly rate just to deal with the Costco nightmare I'm about to bring her. She worked well with the chef Barney. They are friendly and would coexist well. The thing about this part of Michigan is everyone knows one another. And all the native Michiganders who make all their money this time of year are hustling to get more money from the summer people.

I began thinking I won the lottery when Paul arrived.

"Switch me places," I told him.

"Uh, no. I'm driving," Paul insisted.

"No, darling, I am," I rolled my eyes and teased.

"I adore you getting cheeky with me. This doesn't bother me," Paul said.

"Just keep your pants on."

I adjusted the seat and started the car.

"It's a manual."

"Don't worry. I can drive a stick, Paul."

I could see him preparing to say "I know you can," but he stopped short.

"So what is a Costco?"

"It's a store. Do you have the I-Pass thingie?"

"What?"

I looked up and saw the transponder.

"The thing that does the tolls?" Paul asked.

"Yes. We're going to Indiana and we're getting on the toll road."

We do just that.

"Oh, going *east* of the La Porte exit. It's bloody exotic. I'm on a pleasure cruise now. So posh and French," Paul joked.

I laughed.

"See, you're warming up to me."

"I still find you immature and annoying, but sometimes you can be charming."

We made it to Costco. Paul was overcome with childlike amazement at the sights and smells. It was a wonderland. I yelled at him to grab a cart.

"A cart?"

"A cart," I gestured wildly.

"A trolley?"

"A cart."

"A trolley."

I was exasperated. "We call it a cart. Grab one. I'm in a hurry. Just follow me!"

I suddenly regretted asking Paul for help. He was like a kid in a candy store. At first, I thought he was doing it to deliberately anger me. After his excitement over massive quantities of what he referred to as biscuits, I realised this was the real Paul. Instead of frustration and annoyance, I viewed this adoration as slice of life. When would I ever get to take a prince to Costco again? Moreover, when would I get to put one to work helping me?

"These are chickens? Just here? For anyone's choosing?" Paul asked as we approached the rotisserie.

A woman looked in our direction, confused. She didn't know who he was. No one in South Bend expected to see a prince on his first Costco run.

"Yes," I laughed. "God, you're going to get found out, Paul. Do you have an inside voice?"

"You sound like my father. I am being quiet."

"You're not."

"Oh, shit. Can we run to a shop or something?"

"We are in a store, Paul."

"I need to get a drink," Paul said, looking uncomfortable. "Like to take a tablet. I forgot to take my meds."

"Okay. Gimme a sec. They have a café up front." I looked over at a deli employee. "Hi, I have an order under Nordgren for two dozen of these puppies."

"I got one for Northman," he said, confused.

"Yep, that's me," I replied. I should have given him my *other* last name. The guy nodded and left.

"Northman," Paul laughed. "Wait, you got *two dozen* of these things?"

"They feed about six per chicken. We have a hundred people with that preference. We also have a salad which will require shredded chicken. Like I told you, our caterer up and quit. This is going to save our ass."

"That's brilliant," Paul remarked.

"I do this for a living, Paul."

"Well, George did say you all were the best. I am not surprised. Still brilliant, darling."

"Why do you do that?" I asked.

"What?"

"Darling?"

"Sorry, force of habit."

"It's overly-familiar."

"It's meant as a term of endearment. Sorry."

"We're not together."

"I know that."

"Okay." I was satisfied. "I just wanted to be clear."

"Got it. I should probably watch it."

"If you don't want people to think we're together, yeah."

Paul nodded, looking uncomfortable. He was quiet. I didn't mean to hurt his feelings, but I needed him to respect that we weren't together. We weren't. People would start to talk if he kept "darling" me around people in Buffalo Shores. It was a fish bowl and everyone had seen us at the bar together last night. The guy returned with a flat cart full of chickens.

"Thank you so much," I said. "You are a lifesaver."

"Not a problem, miss. Should I send this up front?"

"That would be great, thanks!"

He nodded and another employee rang the thing up, handing me an invoice.

"Okay, next we need some sides." I continued on our mission.

"Mash? In massive quantities?" Paul gasped. "Yes, please."

"Paul, this isn't your wedding."

"Well, I approve, okay?"

We picked up the mashed potatoes, setting more than half-a-dozen huge chafing containers in the cart.

"Asparagus!" I grabbed a ton.

It would do.

We moved onto rolls, Paul delighting in the "Hawaiian" variety.

"Can I get some?" he asked, as if needing permission.

"Fine, whatever. Are you going to get stoned and eat a bunch of rolls later?"

"That's a brilliant idea."

I sighed and rubbed my temples. We took a bunch of chafer racks, more chafing pans, and the lights used to keep food warm. We collected starters from the frozen section. It was the best we could do for finger foods. I lost Paul to an assortment of mini cheesecakes. I caved like a mother with an impulsive child out shopping. Once up front, I split the orders between Paul's things and mine, putting the massive catering order on my expense account. I'd settle this with the father of the bride later. He'd pay me because it was uncomfortable to let it sit there. He'd apologize profusely, but I wasn't concerned. Unlike the catering company's charge account, my AmEx wasn't about to bounce.

"Take the cart—er—trolley or whatever the hell it is." I pointed at the flat cart full of boxes of chicken.

"Who will get the other two carts?"

"I can push and pull both," I assured him.

"That's a talent!"

I ignored him as we proceeded to the car. He had grabbed a massive pop from the café. Paul was like Marie at the store. It was ridiculous, but I had to admit he had made a stressful, awful task less so. Maybe *hate* was too strong a word for my feelings for Paul?

chickens and clandestine run-ins

. . .

paul

I struggled not to intervene as Sanne packed the Mercedes with massive boxes of cooked chickens. She jumped into the hatch, occasionally barking orders from the boot. I didn't mind. That she even knew what she was doing right now was somehow sexy. Maybe that was the afterglow of the evening before? It was also a trip to watch her fix everything for someone she barely knew. She reminded me of Lucy and my cousin, Rita. She wasn't waiting for anyone else to make a choice. As I understood, she was the best lady-in-waiting this bride could have.

"Yeah, I think we're good," Sanne said as I returned from the trolley keeper area. "I put your shit up front under the folded seats. Don't forget to take it out when you get home."

"Got it. Thanks."

I badly wanted to kiss her. It was harder and harder to fight. This was the most ridiculous feeling. She'd made it clear we were *not* together a bit ago. So, I stood firm. No kissing her in a carpark. I wanted to. I fancied her so much. The pull was intense. It was a magnetic attraction I could not explain.

"You doing okay?" she asked.

"Yeah. We can head back."

Her commentary about my voice level reminded me I forgot my meds. I was a bit embarrassed to do it in front of her. However, I had no choice. I stashed tablets of stimulants seemingly everywhere not because I was an addict but because I naturally forgot everything—including the medication that allowed me to remember things. It was a vicious cycle. I rifled through the console, took my tablet, and we were back on the motorway. Sanne didn't ask me about the meds. She did check in on me, though.

"Like, if you're sick, it's fine, but can I get you something?" she asked, voice genuinely concerned.

"No," I answered. "It's... I must take these every day. I'm not sick. I have ADHD."

"Really? Oh. That's fine."

"You're not going to crack a joke?"

Sanne laughed. "Fuck no. Why would I, Paul?"

"Some people take the piss."

"Nah. I wouldn't ever do that. I'm not a bitch, Paul. Remember? I'm not the one who says off-colour things?"

I chuckled. *God, she never stopped, did she?*

"Can you help me unload all of this? I know it's awkward, but it would really help—"

"Of course," I answered. "I wouldn't dare ditch you in this time of need."

"Thanks."

Sanne looked happy. "I do appreciate your help, Paul. The bride will never know who saved the day, but I will. So, thanks for doing it."

"No worries." I smiled. "So, I've won you over?"

"I didn't say that. I can appreciate you a bit more as a person."

"Uh-huh."

We arrived at the hotel to find people milling. An older man in a tux was sweating and white as a sheet. I assumed it was the father of the bride. He surprisingly ignored me. I was grateful. The last thing Sanne needed now was someone mooning over me. She told him to get a drink and relax as we unloaded her secret save-the-day stash. Her assistant rushed over. She looked at me, confused.

"You got it all?" the girl asked.

"I got it all. Susie, Paul is going to help us unload. Just tell him where to go. He can take orders."

I wanted to make a joke about how well *she* took orders the night before, but obviously did not. That would have put her in a bind with her employee. It would have also enraged her.

"Oh… okay," Susie said. "Sure."

I got to work. Susie didn't bark orders. That was a Sanne thing. The woman could be *so* direct. She didn't quit. I wondered if that was the Scandinavian side of her? Maybe that was what did it for me? I couldn't tell. After everything was unloaded, Sanne pulled me aside to thank me.

"I really appreciate it. But I don't want you to lose your cheesecakes," Sanne joked.

I chuckled. "Yeah, not the precious cheesecakes. What do I get as payback?"

Sanne crossed her arms.

"Hey, you said—"

"You're insufferable, Paul."

"I promise you won't regret it."

She quietly said, "I'd be glad to get up to *something,* but I'm not going to be done here until near one and I am staying at my sister's—"

"If they aren't booked, I could get a room?"

"You aren't serious?"

"Look, a repeat of last night is well worth it if you're not keen on doing a walk of shame back to my brother's place. I get it. It seems unprofessional. I'm not suggesting you be uncomfortable."

"Fine," she agreed after a moment. "If you think I'm worth the trouble and you're willing to stay up late."

"I have no plans. Something about a brunch tomorrow at noon. Beyond that, I'm all yours. What else would I get up to?"

"I will text you." Sanne smiled a bit.

I couldn't resist the urge to kiss her. It may have been a terrible idea. I realised this as I bent down and leaned in. She might have slapped me. I would not have blamed Sanne. I was out of line. However, she pulled me in and then pushed me away. She had a cheeky grin.

"Until later," she said.

"I will leave a card for you at the desk," I promised.

Sanne turned and left. I resisted the urge to celebrate as I packed off to my brother's house. He and Pat were back from the game in Chicago. George often flew them into the city. Or rather, he flew from where we were to a regional airport, a moment's drive from the new stadium. Little Charlotte napped on the floor, passed out adorably like a starfish. I struggled to find fault with it. I wished to do the same.

"How does she manage that?" I asked Patrick.

He made a drink in the kitchen.

"Oh, she's so sweet when she's out, isn't she?" he asked. "Got home and just fell asleep like that."

"I saw the game. You played ace." I only caught part, but it was good.

American "soccer" was so strange to me.

"It was alright. Where the hell were you? The barn?"

"I had to rescue a fair maiden," I joked.

"Oh, what now?" George entered.

"Sanne had to save a wedding. She needed a large car to transport two dozen chickens. It was a wild ride. We went to this amazing place called Costco. I got those buns over there. And then these mini cheesecakes."

"Sanne took you to Costco?" Patrick burst into laughter.

"What is a Costco?" George wondered.

"It's this massive store that has everything in bulk. And they have chickens on offer. You just grab them. They smell heavenly. And then all these puddings and everything. And mash to feed an army!"

Patrick shook his head. "You two are so fucking weird. I don't understand your childhood at all."

"I rather liked it. I'd do it again. Besides, the woman knows what she is doing," I said. "She's a bit terrifying when she is telling you want to do. She insisted on driving the G. But, in a way, I don't mind it. What would you call that?"

"Authoritative," George answered. "That is what you're into?"

"I think so, surprisingly. It's sexy as hell."

"You can't shut up about her now. God, this summer is going to be miserable. Don't ditch us next weekend. The polo and all that," George said. "I will curse you."

"I'll ask her to come with."

George rolled his eyes. "Are you dating her now?"

"No. She's pretty clear on that."

"But does that suit you? Because everyone in your family is a serial monogamist," Patrick noted.

"It's fine if she remains like this. I'm going to see her later."

"What?"

"Don't expect me home. Maybe not until morning."

"You are getting yourself into the shit, bruv."

"Are you telling me not to? Is there some moral objection?"

"Don't fuck us over."

"I think that Sanne is a consummate professional. She'd never hold that against you two. You have nothing to worry about. If anything, shagging her has softened her a bit. She flat out hated me until I got her off. I guess that was a bit of magic?"

George snickered. "Uh-huh. I'm sure it was *magic*."

"What? Both of you seem to think you have magical cocks. Or are you just cocks?" Patrick asked, passing me a drink. "It's like a fucking god complex."

"And you love it," George said.

Patrick didn't argue.

I rolled my eyes now. "I don't wanna know. I hate living with couples. I swear. You're usually both so adorable it makes me want to be sick. But this... no. We're not having this conversation."

"So, you're not bringing her back here?" Patrick asked.

"She won't come back here out of some sort of boundary she has set. So, it's another night hooking up at the hotel. Really, that's not too bad for me, right?"

"You're insufferable."

"Funny, George, she just told me the same."

"Well, at least she knows."

"Tomorrow will be interesting," Patrick said.

"What? Why?" I asked.

"The brunch is at Elisabeth's," George replied. "Her mums are hosting."

"What? Why did I agree to that?"

"Because you wanted food," Patrick answered.

"I won't presume she's going."

"I would. It's her mum and it's like five minutes up the road. It's Hannah's birthday. That's Sanne's other mum. I wouldn't imagine your little girlfriend would miss her mum's birthday?"

"Shit," I groaned.

brunch fuckery and bachelors

. . .

sanne

"You know the princes are coming?" Mom asked as we assembled a mimosa bar.

I froze and nearly dropped a magnum of champagne on the back patio deck. *Way to play it cool, Sanne!*

Mom snickered.

"Mom, you could have *told* me! Why did you invite them?"

"Your mother wanted George and Patrick to come up. We invited all the locals. We weren't going to snub her clients. They are bringing their daughter and George's brother."

"Great," I said, voice flat.

"Something you want to say?" Mom asked.

"No."

She made a face like she already knew.

"I made Linnea swear—"

"Linny didn't have to squawk for it to be obvious. Your reaction alone said it all."

"Why is everyone on my ass about this?"

"Because, sweetheart, it's funny. You swore up and down that you hated him and now you've got a bit of a crush."

"It is *not* a crush!"

"What is it then?"

"Well, I'm not going to have that conversation with you."

"What? Why?"

"Because I don't go into detail with you about my sex life, mother," I protested.

It was *not* a crush. I was being honest—partially. I was also being obtuse. Last night, I very willingly went down on Paul before we had sex twice and then once more in the morning. Normally, I avoided blowjobs at all costs. I found them tiring and they hurt my jaw. Plus, men were rarely willing to reciprocate—see my entire relationship with Darren. Paul revved my engine enough to make it worth it. Also, he did that thing again that set me on fire. No, I was not about to tell my mother that he'd once more made me see the face of god.

I would not admit that this was a full-blown case of infatuation. It was more than a little crush. I stayed with him overnight. I didn't do that with random hook-ups. I wasn't sure what we were doing. That was still to be determined. However, we were doing something. I was like putty in Paul's hands or even his mouth. God, the things he could do with his mouth all over my body! It was so good. I was not about to call it. This was the best sex I ever had ever had.

"Well, I think it's fine," Mom said. "You should have a fun summer."

I was attempting it, surely.

When the boys arrived, I acted normally. Linny watched me like a hawk. She was self-satisfied. She predicted we'd end up in bed together. She shared her prediction with Mamma, who then shared it with Mom. They all looked smug. I was not about to let them know that anything changed. It was about *sex*. This wasn't about wanting to start something with Paul. He was an acquaintance who got me off. That was all, right?

"Can I speak with you?" Paul finally found me alone.

I tried so hard to duck him.

"Paul, I'm not getting into anything—"

"No, no. It's about the stag party thing I said—"

"Oh, shit. We still haven't talked about that. Sure." I agreed. "Come on into the house. We can chat in private if that's better?"

Paul nodded. "Honest, I'm not up to anything, Sanne."

He *said* it, but as we stood in the family room, Paul's face told a different story.

"What do you need?"

"Things are a fucking disaster with the stag. It's... we're trying to plan some sort of gay party and straight men... we're useless. Also, they're not interested in a wild weekend. They're old men, I guess. And we're all convinced they aren't. To make it worse, Gerry has been buried under his own stupid wedding prep and he's left so many loose ends."

"You want me to plan a bachelor party?"

Paul winced.

"I cannot begin to tell me how much you will owe me for this."

"I am good for it. I will be so indebted."

"You will be," I groaned. "Paul, I don't plan—"

"I asked Dad if we could use the yacht. It's going to be near the riviera at that time. Nat and Ed are planning on using it."

I didn't pretend to know Nat and Ed as if they were friends.

"They've got time. And now George is *insistent* that Natalie be there, or he'll lose it. She's the best woman. I don't know why we are inviting women."

"You want me to plan a bachelor party... in the Mediterranean? In like two months?"

He winced.

"Using the royal yacht?"

"Technically, it's a *private* yacht. We own it. The Crown doesn't."

"Paul, it doesn't matter who fucking owns it. Also, I can include whomever on the invite list. Natalie and George are twins, so I can almost see it. I'm also a twin, remember? We're a little weird."

"More than a little."

I glowered.

"So, you say you can include them? Does that mean you will do it? Help me, I mean."

"I will invoice you for my services but, yes, I will do your stupid personal favor."

He kissed me unexpectedly. I wanted to slap him. He broke every rule. At the same time, I liked it.

"Uh… Sanne… we're having cake," Linny said.

I pulled back and turned, looking petrified.

"Sure, yeah, uh, yeah," I stammered and caught up with her.

We returned to have cake. Paul tailed us. I was about to hear all about it from Linny.

"Umm… later, I need to know everything," Linny whispered.

"I swear, I want to kill you."

"What is up with you, Sanne?" she asked.

"Nothing. He kissed me because I agreed to help him plan the bachelor party. According to him, it's an epic fucking disaster. He cannot keep his hands off me. He's so touchy-feely."

"Oh, yes, that's awful," Linny snickered.

We sang Happy Birthday to Mom and cut the cake. I ate an alarming amount. Getting a piece of wedding cake remained my favorite thing. I loved cake tastings. It never got old.

The party wrapped up and Paul wanted an explanation of what to expect.

"We're going to have a *professional* conversation," I said. "When can you meet to discuss this further?"

Paul answered, "Tomorrow?"

"I'm headed back today. I have client meetings the next two days in the city. I can't do it until Wednesday."

"I mean, I could meet with you there?"

I facepalmed. "You want to come back with me."

"Is it that obvious?"

"You're so bad at being chill. You are bad, Paul."

"Guilty as charged. I am a naughty boy."

"I could slap you right now!"

I wanted him to kiss me. The way he looked at me made me want to do awful things.

"Fine. I'll behave... for now."

I groaned. "Whatever. Go get your shit. You can stay with me. No sense in paying for a hotel room when we both know what we're about to do."

He grinned at me slyly.

"Don't get like that. I'll pick you up in an hour," I said. "Don't make me regret this, Paul. And bring your planning shit. I am serious."

"Yes, ma'am," Paul said.

Unexpectedly, he gripped my face with both hands and gave me a hell of a kiss.

I stood there, my entire family gawping. I hated him! I swear I did! I wanted him to keep going. He was intoxicating. I wanted more of him. This was the first time that I honestly didn't care who knew we were going at it. I knew the summer would be exhausting—it always was. However, I would spend far too much time fucking Paul. I didn't even hate it. *What the hell was happening?*

Paul left with his brother and Patrick a moment later, adorably holding Charlotte's hand. I hate him for it. Once we're all free and alone in the house, Marie begins the interrogation. I am surprised by her interest in this situation if not mortified by her glee.

"So, are you going to marry him? Will that make you a princess?"

"No. God no. We're not getting married," I answered.

"It doesn't work like that," Linnea said.

"It wasn't a big deal. It was one kiss."

"It was a hell of a kiss," Mom laughed.

"It was a peck," I lied in protest.

"If that was a peck, I do not want to see what a kiss is," Mamma said.

"Well, when you marry him, I want to be a flower girl," Marie declared.

"Okay. That will never happen."

"If it does?"

"Sure, sweetie, whatever." She ran off to play with her tablet.

The rest wanted to delve deeper.

"So, you looked *happy*?" Mom pointed out. "Happiest I've seen you in ages. He makes you nervous."

"He does *not* make me nervous! He annoys me. And it's a bit of fun. It's nothing."

"Uh-huh." Linny laughed.

She had the best time.

"Has he taken you out?" Mamma asked.

"He's booked them a hotel suite twice. Does that count?"

"Linny, I'm gonna kill you!"

"Well, now we know why she's happy," Mom joked.

"I don't find this funny," I said. "It's not funny. We're grownups and I am staying with Linny because two-thirds of my events are up here this summer. I'm not about to bring him back there. Nor am I willing to go back to a client's house to have sex with him."

"So, she admits they're up to something. Here it goes." Mamma was so satisfied with my admission.

"It's more than something!"

"Linny, staaaaahp!"

"I know way too much to be like, 'Oh, it's just a quickie here or there.' She said he made her see the face of god. Those were her words."

"He's fine," I lied.

"No. You insist it's the best sex you've ever had and that he's hung like a horse. So, get over yourself. Spill. I am in a dry spell."

I resisted the urge to call her out on fucking Jeff. That seemed cruel.

"Fine," I groaned. "He's amazing. He's beautiful. He's not selfish at all. He's certainly not boring. God, I hate him. He makes me want to do bad things."

"Sounds like a keeper," Mom quipped.

"He's just fun. We're having *fun*."

"The way you look at him is not a look of *fun*," Linny said. "You two were practically clawing at one another when I caught you before the cake. It was hot. Just admit that you find him super sexy, and you enjoy him. It's unfair to him to act like you don't."

"I don't owe him shit."

"Uh-huh." Linny was unconvinced. "You're staying tonight or headed back?"

I decided to just say what is going on to get them off my back. "I'm headed back as soon as I can pack up. And I'm bringing him back with me. He needs help with that party and—"

"She's now planning the bachelor party."

"You don't plan bachelor parties!" Mamma shook her head.

"Oh, she's weak. She just wants a convenient excuse to see him. She is *weak*."

"Linny, I'm going to kill you!"

"You won't at all. Get over yourself."

I shrugged. "I'm being practical. We'll hook up. Best to just let him stay with me."

"I love you but you're a mess," Mom said. "You're falling for him. I know you. He makes you all silly."

"He is good in bed and fun to toy with," I protested.

"I think it's more than that," Linny said. "And I will leave it there because you'll only argue. I know you."

the welcome home

. . .

paul

May brought busier days. It wasn't only polo matches. There was Gerry's wedding. This was George's first trip home since the disastrous stag trip. He was a bit tail-between-legs over the Lucy-Winston thing. It was for the best. He should have been ashamed. It was probably good for Sanne that I was on the move. She was buried underneath weddings. I couldn't keep up with her schedule. It was nice to have zero obligations apart from amusing George and playing uncle by day. No matter how mad her schedule got, I was there to pick her up.

When we arrived at the castle the Thursday before the wedding, I was in a good mood. Even George's annoying, neurotic behaviour couldn't keep me down. I spent the morning before we left from O'Hare fucking Sanne against the wall of her flat—her idea. She'd been at some sort of reception, came home late, and booty-called. I took a cab far too and got an earful from George about "disappearing in the middle of the night" but it was worth it. I raced home to make our late afternoon flight to

Heathrow. We had to get in a couple rounds before I was gone for the weekend, of course.

If I was being honest with myself, I knew I was wrapped up in Sanne. I thought about her nonstop. I texted her like it was my job. I got off on her being grumpy about something. For her, being resistant was basically flirtation. It was the sort of sexual chemistry I never imagined I would have with another human. Sanne was ideal. I had fallen for her. In a month's time, I was hers. Hook, line, and sinker.

We arrived mid-morning after a terrible commercial flight into Heathrow in which none of us slept. Instead, we all entertained Charlotte in shifts. She didn't realise that sleep was an option on planes. I cannot count the number of episodes of children's programming I cued. At least there were three of us, right? I have no idea how my parents did it with four. It was good practice for George, I supposed. Their surrogate had *officially* fallen pregnant and was due in the new year. I could not have been happier for them. I was glad not to raise an infant at the same time. I enjoyed the carefree life. In fact, I might have been enjoying it too much.

"You look bloody exhausted," Natalie said.

"Look, Nat, none of us really slept," George grumbled. "Planes are hard."

"First of all, they aren't. Second, try flying all day in a G Suit. Third, sleep is for the weak."

"Ignore her," our cousin Nira laughed. "God, Nat, your superiority can be *insufferable*. Not all of us will ever elect for survival training and stay up for five days straight or whatever."

"We could have used you. Charlotte could have, anyway," I remarked.

Dad entered. "Oh, good, you're here! Brilliant. Where is the baby?"

"Patrick took her on a walk. She's wired. We're trying to get her on a nap schedule. It's pointless." George sounded defeated.

"Good luck with that. She's going to have a rough time. Paul, chat please?"

That was never a good sign. My siblings—very maturely—gave off a "ooooh!"

I glared at them and followed my father into my cousin Rita's office.

"We need to talk about your expenses, young man," father used a tone I dreaded.

"Uh… expenses?"

"What are you spending money on? I bought you a bloody car. You live with George. Your mother takes care of the horses. But when my staff got your statements for the last month, the expenses had practically tripled. I asked for an itemised list—"

"Dad, that's mad!"

"Well, so are your expenses! Why are you spending so much on a hotel? Are you having an affair with a married woman?"

I was mortified.

"I don't want to discuss it. Am I exceeding my allowance?"

"No, no, of course not. But people find this… conspicuous. I am concerned, son."

"I am not having an affair with a married woman," I assured.

"Does George not allow you to bring people home?"

"It's more complicated and with their kid… I don't want to impose."

"She has no place to stay?"

"No. No," I insisted. I was offended by his insinuation.

Dad crossed his arms and gave a look. It was the look he gave when he expected a satisfying explanation.

"Look, she has a flat in Chicago, but she stays with her sister —who also has a young child—and we don't particularly want to get into it there. So, when she's in Michigan, we usually go to a hotel. I can get a break in a room if I ask her. Her family owns part of the hotel—"

"That's embarrassing. Certainly not!"

"She's my girlfriend. It's above board. She's not married. I can assure you—"

"That's really all I cared about. You cannot afford a scandal when you are quite clearly *not* working. Have you given any thought to that by the way?"

"I will probably come back in September, yes," I replied. "To help Nat."

"Brilliant. We can start scheduling things upon your return."

"I know you think I'm useless," I said, "but I'm not trying to be. I just don't think it's fair that Nat gets all the support people and help in the world. George is left out to dry while he and Patrick are trying to figure all of this out. I am just trying to help—"

"And your mother says that by all rights you are helping them immensely. It is admirable. I don't know many men who would be willing to do that. You're doing fine."

Father pats me on the shoulder. "Keep your nose clean and come back in the autumn and we won't ever have to worry about anything."

If only it were so simple. I'm worried about September. I was ninety per cent sure that I was doing the right thing in coming home. Unfortunately, the more invested I got in Sanne, the more I wanted to spend the rest of the year in America with her. As soon as I left, her season would slow. I have her undivided attention by November. I only wanted to relish her with affection. I had no idea what was happening.

"So, she's American?" father asked as we left the office.

"Yes." I hoped he didn't razz me.

He had absolutely no room on this issue, given that Mum was raised there, and he preferred American accents.

Sanne's accent was not why I had fallen for her. It was lovely, yes. It was a plus. In the words of my indelicate older brother, fucking Americans was something everyone is primed towards. It's like fucking a pornstar. George believed it came from conditioning. I worried we were genetically defective. It had to be the inbreeding.

Initially, it was Sanne's completely indifferent view of me—and previous hatred of me—that made me desire her. She liked me now, but was resistant to commit to anything. Somehow, it made her twice as hot. Again, I was a people pleaser. She struggled to be vulnerable. The moment I could test out her vulnerability and break down those walls, I felt superhuman.

It wasn't just that, either. She wasn't like me. She was superhuman and motivated. She always knew how to fix something. She could give orders and solve any crisis. I couldn't put my finger on why that made me want to confess everything to her, but it just *did*.

Dad only said, "Good, good."

"It's a summer thing." I lied to calm us both down.

"It's fine, Paul. Either way. Things can get quite complicated. Ask me how I know," my father said.

We arrived back in the drawing room, where everyone else was staked out. Our Mum rushed over.

"Oh, there you are. You're tan!"

She gave me a hug with her free arm. Charlotte on her other hip. She was, as expected, completely absorbed in her granddaughter.

"I am, yes," I said. "The sun has come out. Running on the beach is nice. It's not freezing anymore."

"Sun. What is sun?" Winston asked.

"I know, right. It's quite unnerving that sun," I laughed.

I notice that he's there with Lucy, looking like a shell of herself at this point. She looks downright ill.

"Luce, you alright? Long time no see," I said.

"She's fine. Leave her." Natalie is quick to step in on her behalf.

"I'm fine. Just a bit under the weather," Lucy acknowledged.

"Lucy, I hope it was alright that I gave your contact information directly to our planner," George said. "She said she called yesterday and that you are starting an email thread… whatever that means."

"Oh, she was great," Lucy said. "The minute she found out I was from the 'burbs, we had to compare notes. We had a good time chatting, honestly."

Natalie looked annoyed. Was she jealous that Lucy and Sanne got on like a house on fire? To be fair, I wasn't surprised. They were similar. They grew up close by, but I suspected their class differential would have been a serious dividing line back home. I tried not thinking about such things. Of course, it is easy to say that when you were me.

"Lucy, you really do look ill. Are you sure you *are* okay?" George followed-up. "Because I do not wish to fall ill."

"George, drop it," Natalie cautioned.

"Sorry," George listened to Natalie alone.

"I'm fine. Actually, Winston, your mum suggested we should take care of the wine thing… whatever that is?"

"It's just the wine for the party, Luce."

"It's our job now." Lucy pulled him along.

It de-escalated things.

Natalie doubled down. "It's none of your fucking business, George. What do you care?"

"I was worried about her health."

"You were out for goss, George," Patrick said, flatly.

"It explains the fast wedding, you must admit."

"She wasn't pregnant when they married," Natalie insisted. "And it's none of your business if she is or isn't. Drop it."

"You're right. It's… fast."

"As is an engagement to your old paramour and two kids within a year and a half after coming out," Patrick said to George. At least someone here was reasonable.

"Fair," George groaned.

"If he takes a swing at you, I won't stop him," our father said.

"Nor would I," Patrick laughed. "I would have handed a teammate their arse over such a comment. It's fucking stupid,

George. Stop bothering Winston—for everyone's sake but especially Gerry and Sheena's."

"I suppose I should go congratulate them and apologise—"

"No, no," mother said. "Leave them be. If she's pregnant, Lucy is in the most precarious place. She's paranoid about losing the baby. She's all over the place. Leave her out of it. Ignore them."

Patrick nodded.

I shot George and Patrick a text,

> Don't share your news about the surrogate.
> This is definitely not the time. Nor will it help.
> Leave babies off the table.

Patrick sent a gif in agreement. George nodded. And, to his credit, he dropped the issue. Maybe we were growing up?

feelings

. . .

sanne

Paul left town so I decided to go out with a couple friends in Chicago after I closed out a wedding. I left two assistants to wrap up with the venue. We wound up at a bar in the Viagra Triangle, known primarily for its ability to attract wealthy older men seeking younger tail. I was along for the ride. There was live music, and the place was hopping. One of my old grad school friends was fresh off a breakup and preferred older guys. It wasn't *all* older guys, but people our age were in the minority.

Given I spent the last month and a half going at it with a twenty-five-year-old prince, I had little interest in a rich fifty-year-old. Turns out, I have a high libido when my partner can keep up. Still, we ran into a few younger guys probably in their mid-thirties. For me, that was ideal. One, Owen, was particularly handsome. We had chemistry and hit it off.

I was free to peruse. I made it clear to Paul that we were *not* exclusive. Who was I to turn down a good thing? I let the guy kiss me. It was nice. It was almost too hot to switch gears. I wondered if this might throw Paul into some act of fabulously jealous competitive sex or if it might make him hate me. The more I made out with this guy in a corner at the bar, the more I couldn't stop thinking about Paul.

That was the problem. I compared him to Paul. Everything he did was measured against how well Paul did it. I tried to shake it, going home with him. We continued things on his couch, saying we were meeting up for a nightcap. I kissed him more. He ran his hand up my dress and I tried to get out of my head. It felt wrong to go through this suddenly. I hated Paul more than ever. He was living rent-free in my mind. All I could think about was how much I wished this were him and not Owen.

"Sorry, shit," I pulled away. "I'm on my period. I forgot."

He looked confused. I was *not* on my period. That had been the case a week and a half ago. Turns out, that unlike 99% of men who found this to be a dealbreaker, Paul didn't give a shit. That surprised me. Maybe British men were less squeamish? I didn't know.

"Oh, okay. Well, maybe you could just give me your number?"

"Give me yours," I lied. "Maybe we could meet up next week?"

I just wanted to get out of there.

I took his number, called a car, and jetted the hell out of there. It was nearly three. I realized it was nine in London. I couldn't help but text Paul.

Want you home.

I fell asleep in my apartment, waking around noon. Linny texted about helping get Marie to and from camp the next day. I ignored that for now and scrolled to Paul's reply to my text. I'm now cringing. *Why did I send that text?*

Is it home now?

> That was stupid. Home for me.

> I could go for you right now. Always. I'll be home soon.

Home. God, what was that even? I lived in two states. He lived in two states and two countries. What did that even mean? And, yet, we made it work. I caught feelings. I caught them *bad.* This was supposed to be my hot summer rebound. I turned down a potentially better-suited guy all over this other guy I swore I didn't even *like* that much. The problem was that I did like him. I didn't just like him. I wanted him.

I wound up back at my sister's a few hours later.

"Yes, I can take her to camp," I said.

"Okay, good. You're a lifesaver. I really cannot keep up like this with the babysitter so unreliable. It makes me pull my hair out."

"I know. It sucks. Well, it appears I will here for the next couple of months, so I'm going to be around," I said.

"That is a blessing, yeah."

"So, I had a realization last night. I went out after the wedding and went home with some guy."

"Oh, really? Do tell. This is because The Prince is gone?"

"I mean, I guess it was? I was bored. Plus, I had friends going out."

"So how was the sex?"

"Never happened."

"What went wrong?"

"I couldn't even fuck him with the foresight it might make Paul jealous—in a good way," I winced.

"So, you finally admit that you're hung up on Paul."

"The Prince is winning. He's not a frog. He's a prince. God, I can't even call him The Frog anymore. Everything we did, I just wanted Paul to do to me—better. I made an excuse and I left."

"What excuse? You had to wash your hair?"

"I was riding the wave."

"Good card. That shuts it down."

"Well, sometimes. Didn't with Paul a bit ago."

"The two of you are terrible! What have you done to him?" She laughed.

"Him? What about *me*? What the hell is this, Linnea? What have I become? I sent him a text that I wanted him 'home' earlier. I was drunk. That was it, I swear. But he asked me if it was home now. And then said he'd be home soon. What does that mean?"

"That the two of you are dating. Obviously!"

"Or just horny."

"Well, yes. You are horny. The two of you have sex more than any two people I know. Damn. I don't know how you aren't broken into pieces. If I got up to that much, I'd be unable to walk."

"He's so good, though. You wouldn't throw him out of your bed."

"I doubt I would. But he's not up for grabs. He's *yours*, Sanne."

"That's ridiculous."

"Is it? Was this other guy attractive? Did he appear normal?"

"He was cute, actually. And he had a nice place, a job. He was normal as far as I could tell."

"But you didn't want him. Not even willing to have a fun evening? Yeah, you're hook, line, and sinker with Paul. Get over it. Embrace it."

"It's going nowhere. He will go home in September and break my heart. It's bad news."

"Um, hello, or it could great? You can't choose when it happens or how it happens."

"Linny, I have dreams. I am building my resume up for a massive job. This is my year to manifest change."

"I think dating a prince is definitely a *change*."

"At work, Linny. Not in my love life. I have set that aside—"

"Have you?" Linny asked me, arms crossed. "Sanne, you are so clueless. You are happier than I ever saw you with Darren. You are laughing, smiling, and you don't want to hide this stuff—even if you insist on it. You are falling for this man. Let it go."

"It's such a bad idea!" I shook my head, put it in my hands, let out a long, frustrated groan.

"I love you, Sanne, but this is no joke. You're so stubborn. You have no idea what will happen in September? That's fine. Live for now."

"Why, so he can break my heart, Linny?"

"Who says he will? Who says something wonderful won't happen? Who says you won't fall completely in love with him and move to London."

"My need to have a job and pay my bills?"

"Meh. You could figure it out," Linny said. "Get over that part and just let yourself have a good time. That is what summer is for, isn't it? Indulging. Give over to your hedonistic side."

I took her words in and looked at my phone. It was late in the UK.

> I'll be home in the evening tomorrow. We should get dinner.

I restrained myself for a minute.

> Sure, but I need more than that. Unless you'll be too jetlagged

> I will tough it out, darling

Oof. Darling? I hated it. I loved it. I wanted him to say it to me. He made me ache.

"He calls me darling. I hate it," I said.

"Paul?"

"I also love it. His stupid, adorable, annoying accent. It makes me want him more. Is that normal?"

"If you're falling in love with someone, yes. You're describing pure infatuation."

"I thought it was lust."

"I think lust changed over to infatuation a bit ago, sweetheart. You're moving towards love. You've long passed lust."

"How do you know?"

"Because you're texting him about you wanting him back home. Because you have real feelings for him. Lust is just wanting to get laid."

"I want that, too. I mean, God. I'm the luckiest woman alive in that capacity."

"Okay, sure, but you sleep over with him. You let him sleep in your place. Whatever you're up to, it's not just having sex with him. It's not a wham, bam, thank you, ma'am."

"I regret that. I think that's how I got this way."

"This way? Sweetheart, you are happy. Sanne, that is good. We're all happy to see it."

"I just broke up—"

"You broke it off for completely legitimate reasons. He wanted to make you a housewife baby factory! You are so much more than that."

"Okay, but what makes you think Paul is any different? Like, look at what women in his family are tasked with."

"Have you ever asked? I think you'd be surprised. His brother is an out bisexual. The King and Queen have supported him, along with Patrick. All appearances make it seem like Charlotte is a member of the family."

"They call her their granddaughter," I said. "That's what Paul says."

"I think you'd be surprised that things might differ from your version of reality. And if they aren't, so what? You were happy, it didn't work, you broke up."

"It took me like three days to recover from Darren and I didn't even love him. I... I-"

I cut myself off and stared at Linny wide-eyed. I was shocked. I shocked myself.

"You love him?" Linny screeched, practically jumping up and down on the couch.

"I didn't say it!"

"You almost did. You would have!"

"I think I was just lulled into something."

"You protest too much. You're in love, Sanne! This is different. I can tell. Oh, God, I'm so excited for you!"

"I'd be more excited if you got more out of that contractor of yours," I said, deflecting.

"Don't make this about me and my contractor. He's great, I'll grant you. Honestly, if you could take the kid to the city overnight, that would be great."

"I could do that," I admit.

"You'd be the World's Best Aunt again. But this isn't about me. You're not getting off so easy, honey. No. This is about you and this man you're *in love* with. I want it for you."

"I want it for me, too." I finally admitted it. "But I am definitely in no shape to *tell* him."

"I think if you told him tomorrow, he'd say the same."

"No way!"

"There is only one way to find out."

"Oh, I'm not doing it!" I shook my head.

"I give it a month before it slips."

plenty difficult

. . .

paul

"I think we should just date," were the words out of Sanne's mouth.

We were catching up at dinner. She paused before letting that out.

I stared across the table, dumbfounded. "Uh, sorry, can you confirm that you just suggested we *date*?"

"Yes, Paul. Jesus!"

"So, let's clarify what that means—to you?"

"God, why are you so insufferable?" she scoffed in protest.

She always let me know I angered her in some way. I didn't really. This was bravado.

"Sanne, just answer it."

I pushed back in my chair, loving the way she shot me daggers. It made me want to wipe her cross look away with a kiss.

"To me, it means we're not seeing other people and if you want to be all cheesy and call me your girlfriend, you could," Sanne said.

"I already did to my dad, so that would be fine."

"What?!"

"Relax. He thought I was up to something dodgy, Sanne."

"What?" Sanne looked confused.

"The hotel bills. It's fine. It's not a money thing. It was a red flag to accounting. He thought I was having an affair with a married woman. I assured him that you weren't married or up to anything nefarious, just that neither of us felt comfortable going back to the other's family's accommodation."

"Oh, great! Now he thinks I live with my parents—"

"No. I told him you flit back and forth and that you help take care of your niece. Also, we all live in my father's houses. One way or the other—everyone but George, I guess. Being a royal makes 'living with the parents' essential. Even my older sister does."

Sanne shrugged.

"I am glad to do all of that. I am all too happy. You're wonderful. I adore you. But royals don't date. And there are protocols for everything—"

"I don't care about that. I'm not about to move in with you in London," Sanne said. "That is neither here nor there, so you don't have to worry about me unless you think the press are going to show up."

"There is a stupid policy regarding state occasions and weddings… things like that. It's 'no ring, no bring'. My father broke it quite a bit with my mother but… he is the world's biggest hypocrite. My mother is untouchable and, as far as he is concerned, superhuman. She's exempt."

"That's actually really sweet," Sanne said. "I love that."

"Okay, it's annoying… my point is that I can't just take you to the wedding and do things like if you were my girlfriend and I was a normie."

She guffawed. "No worries. I can't be a guest. I'm the ringmaster, Paul. So, we don't even have to bring it up if we don't want to."

"Okay, cool."

We left, taking the same suite we've gravitated to. I found myself happier than I had been in ages. Exclusive was a thing—a big one. Given that Katrine mangled my heart last year, I was nervous to hop back into anything. Or, at least, had been.

We fucked on the couch. I struggled to last, listening to her scream my name. It was torture. She was just too wonderful. The way her hair bounced and her face flushed did it for me. They way she gave herself over to me now, exclusively, made it sweeter. As we were falling asleep, both sweaty and sedate after yet another bout of fabulous shagging, Sanne noted that she was worried *I* might break *her* heart.

"I dunno. I guess, you're living so far across an ocean. And what if I take a job somewhere else. I worry that I'm not being honest with you, Paul."

I shook my head. "I'm not worried."

"Why?"

"One, this is so far down the line, we have no business worrying about it."

She shrugged. I worried I would offend her.

"Two, I've done the long-distance relationship thing before. It's not the end of the world. Not preferable, no. I think we could be fine. Again, too soon to worry about that, though."

"Really?"

"My ex lived abroad. In Europe, things are less complicated, but our lives *were*."

I prayed she didn't drill me with a half dozen questions.

She smiled. "Oh… okay. Yeah, well, that's fun. Maybe I could just move back to Norway."

"Move back?"

Sanne answered, "I was born there. I spent the first three years of my life there."

"Really?"

"Yeah. Things were easier for our mothers. Plus, Mamma wanted to ensure we were eligible for Norwegian citizenship.

And since we needed her and to be born there, we accomplished both. I have American citizenship, too."

"That's fascinating," I said. "My mum was born in Wales, left the UK when she was five, and came back many years later when she met my father. Maybe you will just move to Norway and marry my cousins' cousin?"

"Who is your cousin's cousin?"

"The Crown Prince of Norway," I replied. "Olav."

"But is he hot? And does he tend to wander around shirtless at inopportune moments?" She giggled. I couldn't help but adore her.

"Oh, that hit you in the feels. I should try harder to be difficult, shouldn't I?" Sanne asked.

"No, I think you are plenty difficult, Sanne."

She blushed. I am surprised I've gotten a laugh *and* a blush out of her in the same conversation.

"What are you doing tomorrow?" I asked.

"It's a day off for me. I wasn't going to insinuate myself—"

"Insinuation flatters me, Sanne."

"Everything flatters you, Paul."

Sanne flipped her hair over her shoulder. She did it to rile me. She held all the keys, per usual. I tried not to react.

"Well, I wasn't up to much. I was going to look at the horses. Up by your mums' house. Fancy joining me? I just wanted to get a quick ride in. George is being lazy. He claims jetlag is about to end him."

"So why do you have to work extra innings then?" she asked.

"Uh, George is the better rider—by a mile," I said.

"You admit he bested you?"

"Darling, any idiot could tell he is the better rider. But, it's pointless. Natalie and Kiersten would take both of us down any day of the week if they were to join up. Natalie is downright fearless. Kiersten is just wild on the back of a horse. I have a healthy fear of things. George is cocky. I'm neither cocky nor brave."

"You're not cocky?" Sanne giggled.

"No. Not like he is. He's always been like that. That's what being born in first place does to you."

"So what does being born third do to you?"

"You already know the answer. I have a question, though," I said, deflecting.

"No, you answer me first."

"Fine. It makes me the youngest child who magically became the middle child when Kiersten arrived. She wasn't planned—at all. I got usurped. I remember being very cross with my parents for years. But, generally, it meant that I could float between my two older siblings and my darling, accomplished baby sister with little issue."

"You were able to float?"

I nodded.

"Fair. What is your question?" Sanne asked.

"I want to know who was born first—you or Linnea? You two never talk about it. I supposed you would. George and Natalie go back and forth about this all the time."

Sanne curled up on my chest. It was nice.

"George and Natalie were born minutes apart and worlds apart, right? No high stakes here. Who do you *think* was born first?"

"Her."

"And why?"

"You're ambitious."

"That's a first child thing, Paul."

"No, it's not just ambition for its own sake. That's a first child thing. No, it's for the others around you. You are always pushing to help everyone out. Your ambition is family, then you. In fact, I'd argue that you have put your own ambitions on hold for everyone else. You have a chip on your shoulder over it. You love to bail people out. But will that make you happy in the end, Sanne?"

She fell silent, looking at me. She slowly shook her head. I didn't know if I'd fucked it all up.

"Okay, fair, I do put others first. I am out for blood when someone says something unkind about my family or slights us."

"You're your sister's bannerman. I get it."

"Her *bannerman*?"

"This is what Natalie always said to George. It's like a knight that follows you around with your colours. Natalie is the brute who always showed up for George. I know, it's funny. It will be even funnier when you realise that Natalie is tiny in comparison to me. But I'm a lover, not a fighter. Natalie could snap your spine. Or shoot you. Or literally take you out in a dozen ways. And now she's the one."

"So does that make you *her* bannerman?" Sanne asked.

"I dunno. Depends on if I go back, I guess?"

"And will you?"

"I told Dad I would after the wedding."

"Oh, sure," Sanne's voice signalled genuine disappointment.

"Don't pretend you'll miss me," I joked, being self-deprecating.

"I don't want you to go, honestly. Not that I have any right to tell you what to do, Paul. But I think I will miss you. I already did."

"I guess you did," I murmured, feeling sleepy.

"I'll miss you. Of course, I understand what it is like to be that person—the one fiercely defending everyone. I'm the bannerman."

"I know," I chuckled, my eyes heavy.

"I was born second," Sanne confirmed. "You called it."

"I know." I smiled.

backseat driver

. . .

"I really don't want to go home," I grumbled and boarded the car with Paul.

"What? Why?" He whined.

"I have dinner with my moms. They know I'm here to stay and Linny outed me. I was planning to see you tonight—"

"Well, I could go with you *to* dinner," Paul offered.

I shot him a look that could kill.

Paul started the car. "What? You and I are *dating*. Should I not be invited to dinner, too? Or, were you going to be difficult and not tell them?"

"I think there is little point in arguing over this."

"What?"

"With you, Paul. With them. They are convinced I'm wrapped up in you."

Paul chuckled and threw the car into reverse.

"I love my mothers, don't get me wrong," I continued. "But having them to myself leads to a tag-team of questions about life choices."

"Well, if I'm there, they can't ask you too many questions. I can answer them myself."

"You think you're the right one to answer them?" I asked.

We left the pricey barn where George and Paul kept their primary riding horses. There were barns in two states. The horses here were more for the sake of fitness. Even as a former horse show girl, it was a bit much.

"You can take the piss all you want but it's easier if I'm there to just settle that concern."

"You really think the world revolves around you—"

"You really think they won't badger you?"

I didn't argue. Paul was right.

"You get off on meeting the parents, then, Paul?"

"Nah," Paul answered. "I got off on the idea of having you all to myself while your sister was out of town with Marie. But that dream is dead if you don't invite me to dinner."

"It depends on what you propose right now, Paul."

"For what?"

"Why should I give you my evening?"

"I have to prove it to you?"

Oh, I wanted to see where this went. He was obsessed with proving to me that he had some sort of plans to get me off. That was the gauntlet I laid down.

"Yeah, you do," I answered, biting my lip. "Prove to me that I should give you the evening when I have to be up for an early consult tomorrow."

"I would right now."

"Turn right up here." I pointed.

"What? Why?"

"Just turn right."

"It's a bloody field, Sanne!"

"It's a dirt road. Just do as I say."

"You love to bark orders, darling."

"You love to take them, Paul."

He knew I was right. Paul turned onto the dirt road. We ended up in a row of vines.

"Just drive down to the valley ahead," I said.

"It's a winery. Where are we going, Sanne?"

"It's a winery. A friend of ours owns it. We host a lot of weddings here in the fall."

Paul proceeded to the valley.

"Put it in park," I directed.

He did.

"And turn it off."

"Sanne, what are we doing?"

"I dunno. What do *you* want to do?" I asked.

He kissed me, launching his lips into mine. It's not like we already hadn't gone here this morning or that we wouldn't later in the evening. Neither of us could keep our hands off one another.

"We really, really shouldn't—" Paul pulled away.

I shrugged. "I mean, I don't mind if we do."

"And if we get caught?"

"We won't. No one is coming out here right now."

We took things to the backseat, pulling things back to the studs, as was necessary to move things along. It was exhilarating. This wasn't the first time I'd had car sex, but it was the most fun I had in ages. It was almost out-of-body. Something about it was so enjoyable that I disconnected. In fact, should someone have stopped to bang on the car windows, I probably would have told them to fuck off. I felt like other than when I was climaxing, I maintained eye contact with Paul the entire time. It was intense and raw. It was exactly what I needed. I just didn't *know* I needed it.

With Paul, when you didn't think it could get better, it did. I wanted to hate him. I wanted to say it was a passing fad. However, the more we did this, the harder I fell. I wanted so badly to say it was meh or that the magic wore off. It hadn't. That is what got me into trouble. It wasn't getting caught out fucking on someone else's property. It wasn't public nudity. It wasn't even the noises. It was trouble for me by me.

I flopped onto the seat as Paul fought his pants at light speed. I was almost fascinated by how in the bright light of day, his ass was about ten shades lighter than the rest of him. Still, I didn't mind the view. I only became annoyed as I sat wondering if he could at least toss me a few napkins. We came wholly unprepared for this liaison.

"Hello, any help?" I was annoyed. "I mean, I did all the work."

"What?"

"Napkins, Kleenex, a god damn towel?"

"Oh, shit. Wait... you're on the pill, right? Shit, shit, shit!"

He handed me napkins from my favorite coffee place. Oh well, it would do.

"Hey, calm down. I'm fine. Implant. We're good. I wouldn't have even tempted fate otherwise."

He grimaced.

"Paul, it's fine. What, do you think I'm like... a mess or something? I don't—"

He shook his head, "No, no. It wasn't a judgement on you. Past baggage. I must be so careful. And anyway... are we going to discuss what you just said?"

"That I wanted a little help to deal with the deluge?"

"No." Paul climbed into the front seat as I pulled on my jeans and shoes.

"Well, what is it then?" I climbed through to the passenger's seat.

"You just told me you loved me," Paul said.

"What?" I gasped. "No, no. You must be—"

"So, you just do that to every guy when you're cumming or—"

My face flushed red hot.

I shook my head. "God, I... fucking Linny!"

"What?"

"Linny said I would do this!"

"Do what?" Paul asked.

"Tell you I loved you. Within a month. It took less than a week. Fuck!"

"So, you did mean it?"

I crossed my arms. "Drive. If you go down the row, you'll come to a cross in the lanes and you can turn around."

"You don't want to talk about it?" Paul put the car in gear and took off.

"I just... I don't need you getting all weird about it. You're being weird."

"I'm not being weird," Paul said. "You told me that you loved me."

"I was in a period of ecstasy, having an out-of-body moment, and I... yes, okay? I think I may be in love with you. I also hate you," I said.

Paul chuckled, turning the car towards the road, "Well, in that case, I love you, too, Sanne."

He annoyed me.

"Don't make fun of me."

He downshifted and put on the parking brake. We sat there for a moment before he leaned over and gave me this long kiss. Paul then put the car in gear and drove off.

What the fuck is happening? I sat there, waiting for Paul to speak. Why did he kiss me? What was going on there?

"I love you," Paul said.

I wasn't sure if he was joking.

"I do love you, Sanne. I'm not cross with you—"

"Did I really say it? Or, is this one long game?"

"Sanne, you don't believe me? Do you not love me?"

"I... I think I do. But don't make fun of me!"

He squeezed my leg and said, "I'm not. Sanne, I find you irresistible. You're lovely. I love you."

"I love you, too."

Shit! The words fell out like a pumpkin off a wagon. I wasn't sure what to do. I couldn't get it back in or reunite it. He smiled to himself in a way that made me want to scream and kiss him. What in the fuck was wrong with me? I did love him. The more I thought about it, the more my out-of-body admission made sense to me.

"What? Are you ashamed to admit it?"

"It's silly," I shrugged. "Paul, I do think I love you. I do. But it's ridiculous."

"What? Why?"

"Because you're an actual *prince*. It's ridiculous. Everything about it is! And I'm not princess material. Nothing about me makes sense as a possible mate for you. I'm like… the worst."

"You aren't. You're accomplished, organized, well-educated, well-spoken, good with people, and relatable. You're brilliant," Paul said. "And you can forget the first part. It doesn't matter."

"Paul, do you think I'm a fucking idiot?"

"No. You're very clever."

"Then *you* know that *I* know that isn't true."

"Fine, I'm a prince. But I'm also just *me*."

"Uh-huh."

"Sanne, tell me everything you know about me. Really. If you can name the top five details about me, what are they?"

"Awkward, hot, far too touchy-feely, loves animals, and great with kids," I said.

"Too touchy-feely? You love a cuddle!"

I glared.

"I will ignore your dagger eyes, Sanne. You just hate to be vulnerable. Except, you really know that you really do enjoy me at the end of the day."

I sighed. "Don't expect me to say it all the time. And if you are thinking I'm going to just fall all over and beg you to stay at the end of this, I may not."

"I get it. I didn't expect that."

"You can come to dinner."

"Oh, really?" Paul feigned surprise.

"We can go back and wash up. Pick me up after you're decent."

Paul smiled, almost too excitedly.

"Why does this appeal?"

"Because I love you. I want to know your family. Is that so bad?"

"We're just barely together—"

"Sanne, I know you love your mums, and they love you. It may surprise you, but I do like my family. We're sort of raised to be like that—for better or worse."

"I have gathered that, yes. You're wonderful with Charlotte. I cannot imagine any other guy your age volunteering to deal with his brother's stepdaughter."

"I have my own reasons for being here beyond that which may be less admirable."

I didn't pry. Paul wasn't ready to share.

"I adore Charlotte. We all do. I love kids. I dunno. I suppose George and I do, particularly."

"It's funny to me, honestly."

"Why? Can men not also be doting uncles or fathers? You are like a second mum to Marie. You love her, and she thinks you are the best."

"I would go to the mat for her. But like… did your dad even raise you? Where did you have that modelled for you? I guess I have a dim view of men in heterosexual relationships."

"Well, you never had it modelled for you."

"The world modelled it in every idiotic sitcom dad or man who has learned incompetence and cannot figure out a damn diaper."

Paul shrugged. "Never thought about it. Even though, I guess my brother and Patrick are a bit unconventional. Their division of labor is unique compared to how we were raised. Yes, Mum was more involved, but Dad did night wakings and changed diapers. My dad loves Charlotte to bits. He adores babies. My grandmother was morally opposed to Dad being so involved. She thought it would harm him in his position or distract him or whatever. Mum expected it of him, and he always stepped up."

I was surprised. "So, do you think Natalie and Kiersten will want that sort of partner?"

"Absolutely. The thing with Nat is, she can't afford to be Mum. That's not even in the cards. Being queen—not a consort but queen in her own right—is difficult. Women always get the short end of the stick there. She needs to marry someone less ambitious and willing to be the primary caregiver."

"And is that even an option? I really feel for her," I admitted.

"I am unsure. Ed is not as intense as Natalie is—few people are. He's retired now and I don't know if he plans to keep working. I suspect they'll be engaged soon. I think he might be willing. It's not totally unheard of. Our grandfather, Keir, was always the primary caregiver when my father and his siblings were around. He managed all four of them. He was the nurturing one. A big, burly Scotsman and, like Nat, a pilot. If he can do it, it can be done."

"Interesting," I said.

Paul laughed. "We aren't all Neanderthals. Our parents wouldn't tolerate it."

meet the mums

. . .

paul

I dressed smart for dinner with Sanne's mums. It was odd. The day started with us in a hotel blowing off steam. We'd gone to the stables. She'd complained about polo being boring—predictably—but she enjoyed the horses. And then on the way back, things took a strange turn. We'd confessed our love for one another after backseat shagging. It was unexpected, but amazing as ever. God, sex with Sanne was always remarkable.

I was excited to have dinner with her mums. I hadn't had much time to say more than a few words to them. In my view, you ended up with your partner's family as much as you did them. In the past, this is where things fell apart. It wasn't necessarily that I made a bad impression, but rather that circumstances between people and their families were off. I read it as a red flag. From what I had observed thus far, Sanne's family was normal. Her mothers were downright lovely. Much like my own, her parents had been together a long time. I thought that was ideal.

"Where are you headed?" Patrick asked.

I passed by the kitchen as he and George made dinner.

"What?"

"You are dressed up," George said. "And you've shaved. You looked like a scruffy mess earlier. Where were you?"

"Went to the barn."

"No, you've been letting your whole routine go because of Sanne. Don't deny it."

Patrick chuckled.

I shrugged. It was true. She dug the scruff, and I grew comfortable with her.

"Where are you going, kid?" Patrick asked.

"Don't be a gossip, Pat," George laughed.

"I'm going out to dinner with Sanne and her mums."

George raised his eyebrows. "What? Are we doing that now?"

I wasn't about to get into the whole 'I love you' exchange. "Well, I may have sort of invited myself."

"Do you do that with all of your hook-ups?" Patrick asked.

I chuckled. "No. We're together. We're dating."

"Dad's going to lose his mind!"

"He won't. He patted me on the back. Apparently, spending money on hotel rooms is no bother but it is a 'red flag.' He was relieved she had a job and wasn't married. Oh, also, she's American, which seemed to mostly make him happy."

"Damn. Does *she* know?" Patrick asked.

"That we're dating? Yeah. She brought it up."

A look of surprise crossed both their faces.

"Don't fuck it up with her mums," George said. "Don't go all awkward turtle and—"

"Best behaviour, bruv. I promise you. Scout's honour or whatever."

Patrick snickered. "You look nice. I think it's sweet. Her mothers like you. Just be yourself and don't go all awkward, like George said."

"You really like her?" George asked.

"Sanne? Yeah. A lot. In ways I won't get into."

"She's a catch, Georgie," Patrick said.

Charlotte screamed, "Papa!".

"My turn," George said. "Have fun. Don't fuck it all up."

I chuckled as I left. He *was* being supportive. George was a dick about my choice of women in the past. I think he thought I was a bit of a fuck up. Let's be honest, I often had been. However, this was about as supportive as he'd get. George only got touchy-feely over his own girl problems—or even now boy ones—but he left those for Natalie. I was the surrogate. I rarely shared such feelings with him. It felt awkward. I was closer to Kiersten. George and Natalie were a matched pair since birth. There was a reason she was his best man.

I picked Sanne up. She looked stellar in a dress that didn't hide her best features—breasts and legs. She dressed conservatively for work, but I supposed she had to. Americans were so puritanical. It was nice to see her less buttoned up. With her hair up, it took everything I had to avoid kissing her neck.

Instead, I gave her lips a quick kiss as she boarded the car.

"You look stunning."

Predictably, Sanne rolled her eyes. "It's because I have cleavage."

"I fancied you in jeans and a t-shirt, too. No, you look pretty. Just take the compliment."

"Next, you're going to tell me to smile more."

"No, no. I'm not. Why are you being so prickly, darling? Also, where are we headed?"

"Just take the highway north like we did before," she said. "And sorry. I'm not trying to be a bitch. I'm nervous."

"Don't be. I promise I'm on my best behaviour, darling."

"I know, I know. You're invested."

I nodded.

"We're heading back to the winery."

"The same place we shagged?"

"Yeah." Sanne giggled.

"Fuck. Me."

"I did already and I plan to later, Paul."

"You're going to run me into the ground," I said. I was glad to try to keep up.

"Well, you can always tell me no, Paul."

"No, I'd rather not. You're lovely. I enjoy you too much. I'll let you know if you're going to kill me."

"I think you're far too young to experience *those* complications," Sanne said.

"I don't think I've ever asked how old you are," I said.

"I'm twenty-eight. I know you are twenty-five since I can google. I'm robbing the cradle. Another reason this will never work."

"My mum was twenty-nine and my dad twenty-six when they got married. It could work."

She was stunned. "Really? Your mom is older than your dad? God, she looks great for being the older one. I wish I had those genes. No wonder all of you are so attractive."

I laughed. "She's always been beautiful. But, of course, she's my mum. I'm partial. She is the kindest person on earth. We were lucky to have her. Me, especially. I think I am most attached to mum."

"That's sickeningly sweet in a way. You look like her," Sanne said.

"I am the only one of us who does. The rest favour Dad. It's funny. The genes run strong. Dad's sister, Aunt Beth, and her two oldest daughters look so much like Natalie it's funny. They all take after our late grandmother. And, obviously, George is a dad clone–if only shorter. Kiersten and Natalie are dupes. I'm the oddball."

"You are sexy as fuck. I don't care who you take after. You're gorgeous."

"So, you can compliment me but I cannot compliment you?"

I turned to see her smirk. Sanne shook her head defiantly. I loved it. I would have kissed her if I weren't driving. We made it to the winery, passing the lane where we hooked up. Her mothers dined on the patio, waiting. We were on time but, as Sanne predicted, they were very early. That was apparently her American mum's doing. Scandinavians felt being early was rude, according to Sanne. They stood to greet us, looking surprised, but not vexed.

"Well, hello," Elisabeth said. "We have one more?"

I blushed, cursing Sanne for not warning them.

"Sorry. I sort of invited myself."

Sanne winced. "It wasn't his fault. I should have told you."

"Well, we certainly don't mind," Hannah said.

They hugged Sanne. We sat as a server arrived. Hannah ordered wine to go with our mains.

"So, are we able to discuss the two of you now or are we ignoring whatever this is?" Hannah asked.

"We're together. We're dating. You can mention it. I wouldn't have brought him otherwise and if he wasn't insistent that he wanted to come and get to know you," Sanne said.

"Why? Us?" Elisabeth chuckled.

"Honestly, I think you both are lovely. I'm grateful for the time."

I adjusted my collar nervously.

The wine arrived, saving me stress. We settled into drinking some dry red, Hannah and Sanne's preference. It wasn't half-bad.

"Well, that's kind," Hannah said.

"This is more dry than I wanted," Elisabeth said.

Sanne corrected her mother's English. "Drier, Mamma."

Elisabeth rolled her eyes and muttered something in what I assumed was Norsk.

"My first cousins are cousins of the Norwegian Crown Prince and his sister," I said, feeling awkward. "It's... different up there."

Sanne's mother pulled a face.

"No, no in a good way." I tried to save myself. "It's nice

because you can just go out and enjoy yourself. They go all over, and people leave them alone. It's a fun time. London is rife with press. It's sort of like being here. You can just relax. Plus, boats. Lots of boating. And it seems small, warmer. Like here. Everyone is so personable."

"No one minds anyone else," Elisabeth said. "Hannah thought it was cold."

Hannah shrugged. "Here they aren't just warm. They are nosey. You're an outsider, an attraction. In Norway, though, I'll grant you, no one cares."

"In a good way," I said. "Everyone minds themselves. No need for unnecessary pleasantries, but when they like you, you know."

"I liked how family-oriented they were. It was nice while it lasted. I was able to land a job up there for a few years. I think it was good for the girls."

"If only one of them practised these days. You are losing it, Sanne," Elisabeth glared.

"Mamma, I can understand you just fine. I assure you."

I snickered.

"It was easier to do all of this in a civilised place," Elisabeth said. "Insemination is free. You just choose a donor."

"We had our own donor already, though. We were lucky," Hannah said. "But for people who don't, it's nearly free. IUI is readily available. It's amazing. Now, we could be on the birth certificate on day one—both of us. The non-gestating parent can be a full parent in the eyes of the law from day one."

"That's great," I said. "I know that George will have to adopt any baby that he and Pat have. That is so bizarre to me. Apparently, surrogacy isn't even an option back home. It's terrible what people must go through to start families."

"Yes, and for us, money was no object. For most lesbian couples, it's different," Hannah said.

"Well any couples—"

"No," she corrected. "Women only earn eighty cents to the dollar. So, that's a forty-cent loss with two of us."

"Thankfully, she is a fabulous businesswoman and we were fortunate," Elisabeth joked.

"Smashing that glass ceiling." Sanne smiled.

"Sorry," I said. "You're right. I've never had to think about any of that. In every way possible, I mean. It is nice not to, I suppose."

"It's challenging but we made it," Hannah said. "And we had two to show for it instead of one. They came out okay, I guess?"

Sanne pulled a face.

"I think they are both quite clever—far more than me, I'd say," I admitted. "At least one of us has our shit together."

"They are both bright," Elisabeth said. "And Sanne could raise an army within five minutes. She's better than I am at managing a crisis. That's why I gave her George and Patrick."

"No crises yet. Although, this bachelor party is going to break me."

"It will be fine when you're actually relaxing on a yacht, though," I insisted.

"Me? I'm not going, Paul."

"What? Why not?"

"First of all, I'm not going to crash—"

"Literally everyone is coming now. Natalie and Ed's inclusion blew everything up. You've done all the work. No one will care. I thought you were coming? Nat is going to fly us from London."

"I don't have time, Paul! I never agreed to that."

"Why? You don't want to go to the south of France?" Elisabeth asked.

"It's four days on a boat and in a villa. I planned it. I regret agreeing to it. Proof I care far too much about you, Paul. I have weddings—"

"Susie, Mark, and I can cover all of that," Elisabeth said. "You mean to tell me that you would refuse an invite to a yacht party with princes and the future British Head of State?"

Hannah chuckled.

"I am not a party person," Sanne protested.

Her words confused me. "Darling, you plan weddings for a living."

"I plan them. Doesn't mean I want to *have* a party. Or be *in* the party. I like being behind the scenes."

"Well, I'd miss you."

Sanne rolled her eyes.

"Sanne, go. I can handle it. What is this wedding?"

"The Donahughs," she replied.

"That's a vowel renewal—Marty and Jim?"

Sanne nodded.

"Oh, I've known them forever. Go, have fun. Be with your—whatever you are."

Elisabeth gestured at me.

"The word is boyfriend, Mamma."

"Well, then go, be with your boyfriend and enjoy the fruits of your labour. Paul, she doesn't *do* bachelor parties. She must really love you," Hannah said, amused. "This is a departure."

"It's more just a party now," Sanne said. "The grooms don't want to be wild and most of the attendees are straight. It is the most hetero thing I think I have ever planned. I think most of the bachelorette parties I have been a part of have been far more miserable."

I chuckled. "See, we're civilised. And that way Natalie won't be alone on a boat with a bunch of men."

"I sense somehow that Natalie, the war hero, is used to being surrounded by men and *I* will be the odd one out. I am not a bro-person. But if I can lie out and drink wine, I'll survive."

"You'll be fine," I assured her. "Really, it's just a party. I turned into such a clusterfuck."

"George *was* near tears. I get it. It was an absolute disaster of epic proportions. Why did Natalie not have her staff manage it?"

"Because her staff—and her expert planner-of-all-the-things —is George's ex-girlfriend. And recently, her new husband and George have come near blows. And now she's pregnant and that... George needs to stop running his mouth like some fragile dickhead."

"What? This is Lucy?"

I nodded.

"Oh. My. God. Well, she's sweet. George does alright for himself. Has a thing for Americans. Do all of you?" Sanne teased.

"I guess George and I do. Jury's still out on the girls. George and Natalie share a type—athletic and tall."

there's no escape

. . .

sanne

I never saw myself lounging on yachts in the south of France. Scandinavians are a particularly hearty people and love a good sailboat trip. My moms had a speedboat attached to their dock. While I was in France, Mamma took Linnea and Marie out on the lake. I loved boats but was unsure what to expect on the royal family's superyacht.

The *Regina* wasn't exclusive to the Brits. I was informed the Belgians used it, too. Paul explained the Belgian King was his Uncle Louis. His father's sister was the Queen of Belgium or something. As an outsider it was all confusing. I walked a rope between staff and girlfriend, feeling compassion for that poor Lucy girl. The other challenge was the insulation that royals built around themselves. I felt closer to the football players on the trip than with Paul's family.

Our party arrived on a private plane to London. Natalie chartered the flight. The bill for this shindig was larger than many weddings I planned. When I spoke to Lucy about charges, she was never fussed. The more I googled, the more I realized that other than her obscenely wealthy heiress mother and her ridiculously wealthy father, Natalie was one of the richest royals in Europe. Apparently, the heir gets some special estate that churns out millions per year. That boggled my American brain.

Googling also taught me without their mother's money and their inheritances, Paul, Kiersten, and even George wouldn't have the same standard of living as their dear sister. I wondered how this division did not breed discord? I suspected it was established from birth and thus accepted? Or, perhaps they were still so fabulously wealthy they just didn't care anyway? All I knew was that if Linny had gotten *all* the spoils while I was in limbo and hoping to simply marry well, I would be fucking angry.

The Villa where we stayed was loaned from a family friend. I expected something cheerful and small. Instead, the place had fifteen bedrooms and a small pool house with three more. Small was relative. This was a palace, but no one commented on it but the footballers. I kept my feelings to myself for fear of being ostracized. I built a life around appeasing the rich. So, I simply put on my "oh, that's nice" face and plodded along.

Natalie, with George as her co-pilot, *flew* us to France on some massive plane loaned from her uncle. She was a ball of energy. I wasn't sure if it was the plane or what. It was sweet. As a twin, I related. I could also see the friction that this caused with some others in the party. George and Natalie were like one person.

Linny and I still struggled to make friends. We were joined at the hip. It ices people out. Even men griped about it. Darren always did. He thought she was overbearing. It's just a twin thing. While Paul is used to it, I got the feeling that Patrick and George's American friends were confused. Patrick and Natalie got along well. To marry a twin and keep the peace, you must be friends with the twin, too.

When Paul announced I was staying with him, Natalie looked confused. I am not sure what they communicated about me, but she was unaware that I was *also* his girlfriend. I was mortified. Paul, in typical fashion, struggled to explain and further embarrassed me. Patrick, God bless him, was quick to convey things and admonish the boys for not explaining. I was still steamed. I could not get over Paul's lack of foresight.

He took our room check-in as an opportunity to get in my pants. And, while I would have normally been down, I was not in the mood.

"I really don't want to," I said, annoyed.

"What? Why? We've got an hour before we eat and—"

"No."

Paul fell back on the bed and groaned. "What did I do?"

"Isn't it fucking obvious?"

"No."

"You're not dense, Paul. You know what you did."

"Can you just tell me, Sanne?"

"Do you find me embarrassing? Do you want to treat me like the help?"

"No, no. Sanne, I'm sorry. I forgot that Natalie didn't know. I didn't think she would care—"

"She thinks I'm here to wait on you. I want to remind you that the planning is done. I did my part. This is your chicken to fuck."

"I am not planning on treating you like a servant. I don't even like the accusation—"

"Paul, I was embarrassed."

"You do not embarrass me. God, you're beautiful. You're smart. I love you. I am not embarrassed. Don't attribute it to malice. I should have told her. I realize that. My Dad knows about you."

"Oh, really?"

"Yes," Paul insisted. "He's the one that matters. Natalie… it's hit or miss. I promise you she doesn't care."

"Uh-huh."

"What can I do to make it up to you, huh?"

Oh, here he went. He knew I would fall like a sack of bricks now. I tried and failed to resist Paul. He pulled me over towards where he sat, grabbing my hands until I was face-to-face with him. I tried to convey my disdain. That was silly. I couldn't get there. God, he was still so hot. Who was I? What was this?

I wrapped my arms around his neck and said, "I hate you. You know that?"

"Yes. I know." He kissed me passionately.

I fell hook, line, and sinker for it. By the time he pulled away, I wanted to climb him like a tree. I have no idea what he did that worked. It just did.

"I think I changed my mind," I said.

Paul grinned. "Good."

I was about to climb on him when there was a knock.

Natalie's voice rang. "Paul, we're having drinks. Whatever you're up to, it can wait."

Busted.

"Nat, we're just changing."

"Yeah, like hell I believe you. C'mon. This isn't about you."

"It's okay," I whispered. "We'll have time later."

Paul rolled his eyes. "Fine."

We heard her walk off.

Paul said, "I'm going to try to put on some swim shorts and forget about your tits for a moment."

"Well, I will be sure to wear a cover up so you can only catch a glimpse of them. I brought the blue bikini."

"Oh, fuck no," Paul groaned.

"What, you *like* the blue bikini."

"I love it. That is the issue."

I rolled my eyes and filed through my bags. Once dressed, we found a spread on a massive poolside table. I'd been told to book a private chef. I hadn't realized how much went into that. The food was good, but sufficiently casual. After lunch, we made the run to the yacht on so-called "tenders". It was like everyone knew yacht language—everyone but me.

The boat, or ship, as people corrected a dozen times—was

even more extravagant than expected. I expected big, but it was a floating palace. Natalie said she'd join me to sun on the bow's sundeck, but never showed. I curled on a lounger with a book and glass of wine. No need to waste time while everyone was bro-ing out. Natalie and I were not going to be besties and had little in common. Oh, well, we didn't need to be besties. We just needed to co-exist.

Since dinner took place on the ship, its crew prepared the massive dining room. I was overjoyed at the concept of a nice meal looking out at the water. By now, everyone was very drunk. We were "happily pissed" as George said. I patted myself on the back for a mission-accomplished situation.

At some point in the late evening, Paul took me below deck to finish what we started. Normal me would have been unable to think about sleeping with a client's family member during an event. Of course, this was different. I planned it out of obligation to the guy I was utterly obsessed with. The drunk-happy vibes added to it.

I figured Paul would fuck me. Instead, what happened was one of the sexiest things he'd ever done. Considering that everything we got up to was hot, this was other-worldly. He kissed me, pressing me up against the wall, putting his hand up my coverup.

"Take these off," he said of my bikini bottoms.

I could have said no, but I didn't. I tossed them aside and continued to kiss Paul like he was the air I needed to breathe. He slid his fingers inside me, rubbing them on my g-spot before pulling away and disappearing. He knelt in front of me and went to town like it was his fucking job. I had no idea anyone could even *do* this with me standing. It was a high I didn't know. I came so fast. I nearly fell over. My legs quaked, my heart raced, and all I wanted was to do it again. I figured if we ever broke up, he was going to ruin oral sex for me forever. No one would top him.

Paul faced me again, then as I stood there, breathless.

"I could do the same," I panted.

"Nah. I want to fuck you," Paul said.

The fantasy of him fucking me against a wall already came true once. And now, here we were again. I admitted I preferred him going down on me with me *pinned* to the wall, but this would do. Paul didn't last long, which was preferable given that we were on borrowed time and there was a countdown clock on being found out. I probably should have felt worse about doing the straightest things imaginable at what should have been a very gay party. Still, my sweaty, satisfied self struggled to feel much guilt.

We emerged into the hall, hearing an argument above deck.

Oh, shit! Time to find out what the hell we missed. the voices grew, the worry that I was about to be scapegoated bubbled up. My work was done, but clients always blamed the planner when things went off book. This was why I didn't handle drunken events like bachelor parties. Things were out of hand. George shouted at their cousin Gerry. Natalie paced. Her boyfriend tried to calm everyone. I felt for Ed. He seemed like such a normal, good egg.

This was going to be a difficult end to night one of this two-night yacht trip.

strippers and
conspiracies

. . .

paul

I was satiated by the time I finished shagging Sanne against the wall of my parents' yacht. I was surprised she even agreed. It was one of those bucket list things like joining the mile high club. Fuck your girlfriend on a yacht. However, this was far more exciting than the mile high club. That was sorely overrated. I wondered if the gods were punishing us for our misdeeds by the time we made it above deck. There, everyone shouted angrily.

I was very drunk at this point, as were most of us. Ed, the soberest, tried to calm Natalie. George shouted at Gerry, something that read as predictable. They rowed like brothers most of the time. I worried it had to do with Winston or Lucy. However, I soon discovered that wasn't the case. First, I felt relief. Then, dread as Natalie launched into a tirade.

"Oh, *there* you are. What on have you been up to?"

I must have blushed red. I looked at Sanne to see her white as a sheet. Natalie glared at Sanne.

"We went… below deck," I said.

"Did you just shag her?" George demanded, annoyed.

"No comment," I answered.

Natalie snarled, finger pointed at Sanne, "I don't know what you are up to here, Miss whatever your name is, but I am unamused by your planning of this charade—"

"Natalie, calm down. What happened?" I asked.

I was hot now. Sanne was already intimidated by Natalie and the odd woman out.

"Did you or did you not organise a stripper?"

Sanne looked at me, bewildered. "No. Absolutely not. I did exactly as asked. No craziness, I promise you. What? There was a stripper?"

"Yes," the lot replied.

"I swear to God, I know nothing about it. Right?"

She looked at me for confirmation.

I said, "Yes, of course. I asked Sanne to help me because I was drowning. Please don't take anything out on her. She only tried to help. She did this out of obligation. She doesn't even plan these sorts of things."

"It's true. He guilted her," Patrick confirmed. "And this isn't Sanne's sort of event."

"She's well-regarded, Nat. Leave her the hell alone," George said. "No, it has to be *this* tosser here!"

George lunged towards Gerry. Ed broke them up. It was humorous to watch George struggle against Ed. His height and massive shoulders made him out to be a wall. George, at five-foot-ten, looked like a whiny child attempting a slap fight, held off by the giant swimmer. Gerry looked nervous at the prospect of Ed letting George go.

"Eh!" Ed barked. "Everyone shut the fuck up! I'm about done with it."

Patrick nodded. Patrick and Ed were the only sensible ones. God, this was embarrassing. Sanne watched in horror.

Ed's voice roared. "I understand the rage over the stripper. However, she left. All is well. I am over this shite! Everyone needs to calm down. Patrick wasn't offended. Calm the fuck down!"

I never heard him raise his voice. This was *some* enchanted evening, wasn't it?

It dawned on me. A *female* stripper. Oh, God, why? The night went off the rails. And I'd missed her? I couldn't even judge whether the outrage lived up to the hype. Ed looked resolute. Natalie now stared at Ed like you might a good steak. God, I hated her right now. The two would be insufferable in a bit. She was mooning like a schoolgirl over him going all aggro-Olympian.

"Now," Ed said, "let's leave Sanne out of it. Who did this? And fucking why did you do it?"

"Gerry did it to be petty!" George bellowed.

"Don't be a conspiracy theorist," George and Gerry's university friend said.

"Gerald," Natalie said, authoritatively. "Did you hire a stripper? And if so, why?"

Gerry was nervous.

"Gerald, do not lie to me or I will go to your mother, so help me!"

Natalie moved to guilt. It would work. Guilt worked well on the Scots.

"I dunno why I did it. I guess I was being petty since you sort of ruined my stag. Also, I thought everyone would get a kick out of it."

"That is the most ridiculous thing I have ever heard!" George fought Ed to get at Gerry.

"Calm down," Ed said. "Calm down, mate. It's not worth it."

"Babe, I'm not offended. It was a stupid prank. I only feel bad that I didn't have enough cash to give her," Patrick said.

The man was downright adorable. I was convinced George never deserved him. He was the kindest sort. He reminded me of mum. He was more worried about offending the stripper than the rest of the damage!

"You were trying to break Patrick and I up!"

"That is a ridiculous conspiracy! George, I didn't honestly think Patrick would care."

"I don't but I found it unnecessary. And again, the poor woman was left without much cash, and she came all this way. Plus, the rush to judgement against poor Sanne because you wouldn't cop to it is fair. Sanne, I must apologise."

"I am sorry. I should have been less combative," Natalie apologised as well.

"Thanks," Sanne sounded diplomatic but still shaken by the whole thing.

"Gerry, you will make sure the woman is fairly compensated in the morning," Ed said. "And I think it's time for us to return to shore."

With that, we waded back home. What a clusterfuck of an evening!

Sanne flopped on the bed at the villa. "I'm never coming on a vacation with you again."

"What? Why? Over that?"

"I just got lit on fire by your fucking sister. She thinks so poorly of me—"

"Natalie is protective of George just like you are Linny. Sanne, she apologised. There's no bad blood. Please just let it go."

Sanne shot me an annoyed look, tossed her clothes aside, and climbed into bed. I followed. She was naked there. I wanted to bother her. I also knew better. I was not about to get lucky. I turned off the lights and turned in, glad we survived Strippergate.

I woke the next morning to find Sanne gone. It was rough waking without her. I'd wanted to tell her it was okay and that I am sorry my sister went completely ape. However, I didn't get the chance. When I went down to breakfast, she was nowhere to be found. No one knew where she'd gone.

"Natalie, what did you say to her?" I immediately went on the defensive.

"What? Who?" Natalie asked, confused.

"Sanne," I answered. "My girlfriend. She was gone when I woke up and I assumed she'd be down having breakfast, but she's gone."

"She's the pretty ginger one?" one of the Man City attendants asked.

"Yes," I replied, my voice laden with annoyance. "Don't be obtuse, Nat—"

"Calm the fuck down! I didn't see her. Did she run off and leave you?"

"Nat, that's not funny," Ed admonished.

"Sort of would be."

"It's not," Ed's voice was sharp. "Do you remember laying into her over the stripper last night? You frightened her."

"Oh, it's fine," Natalie said. "We were all drunk. I yelled at Gerry, too. It's my job."

My voice grew hot, "No, it's *not* fine, Nat. We were drunk, yes, but there is a big difference between you laying into Gerry and Sanne."

Ed nodded in agreement.

"What? What is the difference?"

"Uh, maybe the idea of going from being on staff to being integrated isn't that fucking easy to master," I answered.

"You never even told me—"

"It's not about telling you, Natalie! It's about me really liking this girl—loving her, really—and you frightening her and being totally unapologetic about it!"

Natalie burst into a fit of laughter.

"Look, call me a fuck up all you want, Natalie! I probably am. But leave Sanne out of it. She's a sweet, lovely person. And I do love her."

Natalie didn't have a smart retort, "Okay, so you're serious?"

"He's serious. Back off, Nat," George grumbled. "If I can

restrain myself from hanging Gerry up by his entrails, you can be nice to Sanne."

"It doesn't even take work. She's a sweetheart," Patrick said. "Why she is with this lovable oaf, I don't know. They're cute together. Let it go."

"Sorry. I will... try," Natalie sounded *just* like our late grandmother.

That was the same woman who went on the warpath against her daughter-in-law over insecurity.

"Shit. Sorry," I heard a voice say.

I turned to see Sanne walking into the dining room, her mobile in her hand. "I should have told you I was going out. You look concerned. Don't be."

"He was losing his mind," Natalie rolled her eyes. "He thought I'd run you off."

"Oh, no, sorry," Sanne said. "I'm checking in on a crisis. We have two grooms and one of them has done something... it's bad. They're getting married next week but they caused a bit of a riot on North Halsted. So be glad you're here."

"A riot?" George wondered.

Sanne helped herself to the buffet, "He began dancing on top of a cop car while wearing what my mother described as 'hot pants'. It was... well, the other groom is super pissed about it. This... this is why we don't plan bachelor parties."

"I'm sad to have missed the party," George joked.

"He encouraged a few people to do the same. Apparently, a drag queen was *pleading* with them to get down off the cars. She even used a bullhorn to tell the party to calm down. It didn't work, obviously. There is a video of it online. Some right-wing news sites are calling it the 'Gay Chicago Uprising'."

"God, we really missed out," Patrick snickered.

"See, makes the stripper thing look innocent," Gerry said.

"Oh, fuck off. You're not getting off so easily, Gerald!" George growled.

"So, what is happening?" I asked Sanne.

"Uh, it's four there," Sanne said. "And my mother just bailed him out of jail. He's getting married next weekend—supposedly. But his fiancé is mad. I don't blame him. He's also an alderman so this makes things even harder."

"I thought gay people usually had their lives together better," a football player said.

"As if," Sanne deposited herself into a chair across from Patrick. "Well, we'll see if the wedding happens. I might have a weekend off for the first time in the middle of July since I was old enough to lug a box or hand out tissues. Well, two, given that my mothers are covering the whole thing for me right now. I will never live this down."

"I'll be sure to send your mums flowers or something. I'm the whole reason this went down."

"No. This is on the groom," Sanne said. "Look, last night was… exhausting but only because I felt like I was at work. I'm sorry if I'm a bit low this morning. I'm just exhausted. I work day and night. But I jest. I once had a bride find the groom going down on a bridesmaid two hours before the wedding in a supply closet—in a very nice Catholic church—"

The room burst into laughter.

"They didn't go through with it, right?" Natalie scoffed.

"Oh, no, they did. She screamed at him, told him he wasn't going to embarrass her on that day, and they got married. I was so confused and concerned that even I needed to take a couple of shots to move forward. It felt unethical somehow."

"How fast was the divorce?" George asked.

"They've been married about five years now and have multiple kids."

"Fuck. Me." I scoffed.

"Yeah. The straights are *not* alright." Sanne giggled. "I have never felt so sick to watch a priest power through a wedding when everyone there was more aware of the groom's behaviour than the bride had been until minutes before the ceremony."

"The required question," George said, "is did the bridesmaid stay in the bridal party?"

"She did," Sanne laughed.

Natalie laughed and hit the table. "Oh my God! I would have thrown her out of the church by her hair. Or, rather, I would have had Lucy remove the woman from my sight. And we never would have gone through with it."

"Are you accusing me of something?" Ed asked.

"No, you'd never be so stupid."

"See, Georgie, it could always be worse," Patrick said.

"Well, I did almost propose to someone knowing full-well that I was in love with you just because I wanted to ensure I did everything as I should have. I'm immeasurably glad I didn't—for both our sakes. But I am most relieved because I love you so much, Patrick," George said. "But, no, you should avoid marrying someone who shags a member of your bridal party the day of the wedding."

"I love you, too. I promise not to shag anyone in a supply closet," Patrick said.

"Hold him to that, Sanne!" George joked.

She giggled. "Sure. I don't think I will have to do much. You two are great. No dancing on cop cars, please."

runaway bride

. . .

sanne

When it comes to wedding planning, you have scenarios which are stranger than fiction. Groom-bridesmaid cunnilingus, a mother-of-the-bride setting fire to a bill sent from her ex-husband for the catering while standing on the cake table, a mother-in-law slap-fighting with the maid of honor, and a father-of-the-bride hitting on a bridesmaid while still mic'd for his speech.

My favorite of these to-date was when the best man and brother of the bride ended up in a romantic moment behind a bank of curtains. The problem was the curtains were sheer and uplit. They were also going at it during the couple's first dance. I had to sadly interrupt and tell them to move it along upstairs, preferably. That was my favorite not just because it was the start of something real—I did their wedding two years later—but because people cheered them.

Then, there are the most predictably-tropey moments. Some of which are relatable. One morning in this vein, I was handling the wedding of particularly young bride marrying her college sweetheart. Tammy, the bride, was a sweet girl from a nice family. Her monster-in-law future mother-in-law saw otherwise. The groom's family saw her a poor choice. Her family lived paycheck-to-paycheck and couldn't afford to pay for anything. His was wealthy and "old money" by American standards. They footed the bill. The groom's grandfather was a former senator. Tammy's humble beginnings appeared an affront to the groom's family's basic sense of reality.

On the wedding day, the bride overheard her future mother-in-law talking with a friend, explaining that Tammy was a passing fad. She hoped Tammy wouldn't "taint" Theo, the groom, from landing a "better bred" second wife. The bride, overhearing this, ran off crying. The wedding was taking place on the grounds of the groom's family estate in St. Joe, over-looking Lake Michigan. She had nowhere to run besides a highway or body of water. I quickly followed her upstairs.

With the help of the maid of honor, I held her as she sobbed for nearly an hour. I didn't have time for this. In fact, I occasion-ally looked at my phone to make sure Susie had everything handled. Thankfully, our vendors were professionals and I had my ex-brother-in-law on hand to help if needed. In my entire time as a planner, only two couples ended it within a week of a wedding. There were the two grooms from last weekend while the other called it at the rehearsal when the bride admitted she was in love with someone else and couldn't marry her future husband in good faith. It was heart-breaking. The number of runaway brides and grooms on wedding day who did go through with it and had, to-date, normal, successful marriages was much higher. Cold feet were a real thing.

"I just can't do it if she hates me this much," Tammy sniffled. "I cannot."

Midge, her maid of honor, insisted, "You must, sweetheart. You love Theo. You two are so solid. He loves you."

"He tells me to just accept it and to ignore her," Tammy

sobbed. "I just can't anymore. She is essentially betting against us and he's not willing to tell her to fuck off."

It was so difficult to watch. I wanted to help.

"Maybe we should talk to the groom," I said.

"He can't see me!"

"What if he was just on the other side of the door?" I asked. "He wouldn't see you that way?"

Tammy nodded. I collected the groom, pulling him away from his bros. He'd been drinking, unaware of the panic his mother caused. I told him what was going on. His smile turned into confusion.

"Well, she's just being dramatic—"

"I do not think she is. Your mother said something that wounded her. She wants to talk to you. I think you can put her fears to rest. She loves you. You love her."

"Okay," Theo agreed to play along.

I left them to talk, knowing full well that we had about forty-five minutes before the ceremony. Every second counted. It was difficult not to overhear their conversation. He pled with her to calm down. She was right. He was dismissive of her concerns.

"Look, you can either marry me or not, but my mother should have no bearing on this," he said, annoyed.

"I need you to go tell her that she was in the wrong, Theo."

"What good would that do? She paid for—"

"I am over it. She paid for this, she paid for that. If she calls it off because of that, then we will go get married at the courthouse and it won't change my feelings at all," Tammy said.

I was with Tammy on this. I also assumed he would bite the bullet, do it, and then they'd have a romantic story to tell later.

"I don't want that. I don't want to fight with her on this day. I'm having a good time."

"She humiliated me!"

"You need to grow a tougher skin!"

His words were sharp. They hung in the air. I was near tears just listening and waiting for her reply.

"I can't do this, then. Theo, I cannot marry you."

"Don't do this. There are no second chances—"

"Well, I will have to just take that chance. You deserve a harmonious marriage. I deserve to have a family who accepts me and a partner who supports me."

"Oh, baby, please don't do this. I love you."

"Not enough to stand up to her."

"She's my mom, baby!"

"I can't. I can't."

The bride sobbed through the door like the world was ending. I supposed it was for her. Theo stormed off. I think he was willing to call her bluff. Now, we had to make a choice. Was she bluffing? Did we run downstairs and tell everyone the wedding was off? Did we try to talk her into it? I had to choose my adventure. I always led with genuine care for the couple. They were my clients even if the parents were paying. In this case, I thought Tammy deserved basic respect. Marriage was a terrifying commitment, insofar as I was concerned. Everyone deserved a happy marriage entered into with support. Buried secrets have no place in long-term happiness.

"I really can't. Can you bring me my mom? I need to get out of here. I will need her to drive me. I know she won't desert me."

"I can get her," Midge offered.

She dashed off.

"I'm sorry, Tammy," I said.

"I'm sorry I ruined this all for you. It was a waste of your time."

"It never was. I've loved working with you. I think you're a wonderful person with a good head on your shoulders. I wanted you and Theo to have a happily ever after. I am sorry it looks like that's not in the cards right now. But maybe down the line? I trust that he loves you. I do. I just don't know if he's grown up enough to do the right thing."

"Thanks for saying that," she said. "I really appreciate you being so supportive."

"I am here for whatever you need."

"I just want you to help Theo, okay? Whatever he needs. I will love him till I die, maybe? I dunno. But I can't marry him. Not like this. I just want my mom."

Mom soon arrived and carted the bride off. I returned to tell Susie what we would do. She nailed down the logistics of a "call off". It was baked into an emergency protocol we trained for. This was an incident. We had a response much like a company might respond to a power grid failure or losing their phone lines. You hoped it never happened, but you had to prepare for anything. She ran the playbook. I went to find the groom.

He was in a state of total disbelief upon hearing that she had left. To my surprise, Theo reacted in the strangest, sweetest way.

"Tell my mother we won't be having the wedding. However, I have a request."

"Yes?"

"Is she headed back to the inn?"

"Yes." The bride's family was set up at an inn just down the shore.

"Can you drive me to her? I need to promise her that this will happen—on our terms—someday. I cannot lose her. I have loved her since the day I met her."

He cried. I packed him in my car with a moment's notice, telling Susie to hold the news of the groom leaving—and with whom—until after I returned. I brought him to the inn where he successfully talked her into letting him come in. Theo convinced her to come with him on the honeymoon. He'd paid for it. No need to be married to go. They'd get the courthouse wedding figured out when they were back from Bermuda. His feelings hadn't changed. All in all, I was bursting with happiness when they relayed this to me before asking me to handle their arrangements for a simple courthouse wedding.

I couldn't say no to love, so I decided to do that part gratis once they returned. That was the addictive part of weddings.

They were blissful when they went well. I was invested. I announced the wedding was off and we wrapped things up. Susie, like my best lieutenant, sprang into action making sure everyone could get back to their cars, parked across from the property while I took the ire of the groom's parents. I stayed neutral externally while internally taking care of the bride and groom. They were already on the way to the airport.

I left, fully expecting to be served with a lawsuit. Instead, the father of the groom pulled me aside and expressed how much he appreciated my professionalism. He hoped they ended up happy in the end. At least he was a human being. I climbed in my car before chaos could further ensue. Susie and I left the venue in the hands of the vendors. Jeff and his band for the day were paid either way. He was always a champ at managing angry drunks, so he promised to handle it. Mission somewhat accomplished.

However, as I wandered back to Linny's, I was a bit bewildered. I felt that painful lack of acceptance only a couple of weeks prior when Natalie shouted at me. I wasn't one of Paul's people. The divide couldn't have been wider between our worlds. I climbed into bed by Linny, who read a book.

"What are you doing here? Did it go alright? Why are you home so early?"

"Runaway bride. And then a runaway bride *and* groom. I'll tell you all about it in the morning," I said. "Can I sleep in here?"

"Of course," Linny said, sweetly. "What's up, buttercup?"

"I dunno. It was a clash of socioeconomic status and dickhead relatives. I felt for the bride. And the groom showed up too late. He got her back, but I worry for them. His mother is a toxic pain in the ass."

"Well, that's nothing we haven't seen before."

"Do you think that will be the case for us?"

"What?"

"With Paul? Like, I'm not saying that I would ever marry him, but... will I ever fit in?"

"I think if anyone can manage that shit, it's you," Linny giggled. "You are so naturally prepared for awkward situations."

"But would Paul stand up to his family if I needed him to?"

"I think he would. You don't give him enough credit. You must trust him, Sanne. If you can't do that, you're going to struggle," Linny said.

fallout

. . .

paul

I came home from the stables one evening, finding the lights off throughout the house. It was only about nine. I expected that someone would be in the living room but nothing. I was opening a beer in the kitchen when George padded in and paused. In the light from the fridge, I could see him. His posture made him look defeated. And, given that he was wearing nothing but pants and a t-shirt, I knew something was up.

"You alright?" I asked.

"Can you just... can you hand me one of those?" George requested.

I handed him one. "You alright?"

George turned on the lights and shook his head. I could tell he had been crying.

"I dunno," George opened the beer. He handed me an opener.

"Want to talk about it?"

"I don't know what to say. We... we lost the baby."

I hugged him. "Oh, Georgie, I'm sorry."

"I… I… I'm broken."

"Yeah, that's a lot to deal with, George. I'm sad, too. We all wanted another baby in the house."

"Patrick is just beside himself. He's been in bed all evening. Totally gutted. It's hard to see him like this. He's usually so strong. Everyone will be here for a wedding in a week and a half, and I don't have a single nice thing to say right now."

"You will have a good wedding. You can be sad and happy at the same time, Georgie. You can grieve regardless."

"Nat and her people will be here in five days. Five fucking days before I must look at Lucy."

George teared up.

"What?" I was confused.

"Lucy's going to be here with her huge, pregnant self. It's not fair. She has everything without a moment's notice."

"I'm sorry it feels like that, but it's not her fault, George. She didn't fall pregnant *at* you. And the more you fixate on it—"

"Do you ever think the world is punishing me for leaving her?"

"No, George. It's just rubbish. The world is fucked."

Nothing I said would make George feel fine again. He and Patrick had been in love with this baby. They'd been so excited to see its heartbeat and share pictures of it with the select few of us who knew. It was exciting. Now, it unravelled.

"We only have a few embryos left. What if we never have one of our own. I don't get to be Charlotte's dad in any *real* way. I want a baby of *our* own. I know that's selfish but… I want that."

"It's not selfish to want a family, Georgie. I get it. I want a family someday, too. But you *are* Charlotte's Dad. You take care of her when she's sick and pick her up when she falls. She loves you to bits. To Charlotte, you will *always* be her Papa. Always."

"No one cares—"

"Maybe the government is shit and it's a shame her mother doesn't care more, but you love Charlotte and have since the first time you saw her. That will be all she cares about—just how

Mummy only ever cared that grandpa showed up for her. He wasn't her biological father, but he loved her as his own. You'll see. And you all will have a baby. I am sure of it. I am."

"You really think she will love me that much?"

"I know she already does, George."

"What do I do for Patrick?"

"Support him. Love him. Same as you would want to be supported and loved."

"I just want to… I don't even know," George shook his head.

"Ring Mum."

"It's three AM—"

"Mum will pick up. You know she will," I said.

"I don't want to be that kid."

"If Charlotte rang you about this, would you pick up?"

"Yes. Of course. Without a single doubt."

"Call her."

I knew our mother would answer. There was never a more tireless champion of us four than Mum. She was the most loving person imaginable. And she would want to talk to George. He wasn't about to cry with me, but he'd probably break down on the phone. I wasn't the right person to talk to him right now. I was having a lot of feelings.

George went off to ring Mum. I went to bed but couldn't sleep. I texted Sanne. I just needed someone to talk to.

This is not a booty call. Can you talk?

?

Can I come over?

Yes. But this isn't a booty call?

No

I pulled shorts on and jetted over to her sister's place. Sanne met me at the door.

"The kid is asleep. Linny's on a date," Sanne said. "What do you need? You look upset."

"George and Pat lost the baby. Don't tell them I told you. If they tell you, act surprised. I shouldn't tell you but… it's fucking with my head."

She nodded. I followed her into the living room where we sat on the couch.

"I'm sorry. That's terrible. How are they?"

"George is crying to Mum right now on the phone. Pat won't come out of their bedroom. It's as you'd expect."

"I'm sorry, Paul. I know that was an exciting thing for them and your family."

I nodded.

"And that's why you needed to talk?"

I shrugged.

"What aren't you telling me, Paul?"

"Something happened," I said. "For me."

She cocked her head.

"You can't… you can't tell anyone."

"I'm not going to you. I signed an NDA," she chuckled nervously.

"Even my dad doesn't know what happened."

"Oh… okay?"

"And please don't judge me—"

"As long as you're not a racist, a misogynist, or a homophobe, we're probably okay."

I chuckled at that. "No. None of those. I… um… so I had a girlfriend. It ended badly. It ended in her falling pregnant."

"Okay," Sanne said, confused. "I don't—"

"We were together a while. I was very much in love with her. It wasn't planned. It wouldn't work for four dozen reasons, but still, it was hard. Because she had a moment where she could have been like 'let's do this'. Instead, her crystal-clear realisation she did not want the pregnancy because she did not want me. She planned to get an abortion. It was all very complicated. And... it ended before we got to that point."

"I'm sorry, Paul."

"No, it's... it's okay."

We sat in silence for a moment. Sanne's face looked down. She was knackered.

Eventually, voice still quiet, she said, "Her loss? My gain?"

I looked back at her and shrugged. "You tell me, Sanne."

"So, it's a lot."

"It's stupid. It's just downright dreadful to even think of myself right now. I had all of these emotions about it. I shouldn't. It wasn't my body. She didn't have to tell me. But she did, it happened, and then she broke it off."

"I bet you felt kinda powerless?"

"That's a good way to put it. I do now, too. I can't say anything to help either one of them. I want to make it all better, you know?"

"That's because you love them. Can I interject with my own issue?"

I nodded.

"I had a similar situation," Sanne said.

I looked at her, surprised.

"I was twenty-one—in college. I didn't take my pill regularly. The condom broke and... I was paranoid. I was sure I was pregnant and planned to get an abortion if I was. My period showed up, so I didn't have to make that choice. In contrast, my sister ended up in the same boat and chose to have the baby. That's how she got Marie. I realise she made the right choice for her, and I would make the right choice for me. We can both be right. But the relationship? It wasn't built to last. I wouldn't have wanted to tie us down."

"You never wonder what could have been?"

"He wasn't the right guy. We broke up a couple of months later. We just couldn't keep it going. I went to grad school and moved on. He's married now with a couple of kids. I'm sure he's happier with her. Life is strange."

Sanne looked down the hall.

"No one knows. It's funny. I felt like it was a kick in the teeth. It was all in motion to… end it." I continued.

"That sounds complicated. It's hard to put yourself out there and lose the person you love, Paul. I get it. Sometimes, I worry that I am just not mean to be in love–period."

"I don't think that's true. You deserve love, Sanne."

She smiled. She *appreciated* me. It felt wonderful.

"I bet he was pretty broken up."

She shrugged. "Yeah. Like I said, no one has ever broken up with me to date. I do the ending, but it wasn't right. And maybe someday you can just kick those ghosts aside. If I hadn't broken it off with half a dozen guys since then, I wouldn't have fallen for you. It's terrifying, yes, but I think it's good for me."

"You don't regret being in love with me?"

She shook her head definitively. "Not yet. God, I love you. Like, I worry because I'm invested, you're going to hurt me. I gotta trust you. I'm bad at that."

It was a stunning admission. Sanne was a mystery, but her words were heartfelt. She felt safe. I was relieved to have her support rather than whinging or derision over my baggage. It was difficult for us both to be vulnerable.

"What? Are you having second thoughts?" Sanne asked.

I'd been quiet. She was doubting it.

I tucked a bit of hair behind her ear. "I love you. I am *not* having second thoughts. I'm in denial about leaving in a little over two weeks. I don't want to. I want to stay with you."

"You can't."

"What will we do?"

She squeezed my hand. "I dunno. Figure it out? I don't have any answers. What I do have is you—for now. Question… how do you feel about Oslo in October?"

I laughed. "Sounds dreadful."

"Want to come visit me? I'm going to be up there on fall break with my moms."

"You want me to come to bloody Oslo?"

"How much do you love me?" she winced.

"A lot more than you think I do," I admitted. "Fine. I will come to Oslo if I can."

"No, you *will*. Because you will make it work if you want to see me. I have a job, Paul. We will have to work around *my* schedule."

I nodded. "Sorry. You're right. If I want to see you, I must advocate for you."

"Don't roll over for your parents, okay? If you're with me and we're going to be a team, you need to stand up for me, too. Don't let anyone say anything about me, alright?"

That came as a surprise.

"What? Why? I never would—"

"Look, I watched a clash of socioeconomic strata to beat the band—the runaway bride. If the groom had just stood up to his mother a long time before, it would have been a different day. I hope they're okay, but I worry about her. Her mother-in-law is… insufferable. She thinks that the girl is just lowly and contaminating the gene pool. I don't—"

"No, no," I assured her. "I know you feel like you and Natalie got off on the wrong foot. Natalie is just a bit aggro. She will always be *a lot*, but she doesn't dislike you. And my parents? I am sure they will find you lovely. And no one would dare say anything to you, Sanne. Not if I have anything to say about it."

the assignment of a lifetime

. . .

sanne

Sanne the Girlfriend was a different beast from her counterpart, Sanne the Wedding Planner. One was fun and carefree. The other was wrapped up tight and wanted abject perfection. The Planner was organized to a fault. People respected her. She'd cultivated a healthy fear even with the squirreliest vendors or most disagreeable mothers-in-law. The Girlfriend was liked by parents, but often mistaken as a sweet, simple thing that basked in bridal gowns and flowers.

I loved scandal and fixing things much more than roses or tulle. People assume coordinators got into the wedding business out of some sort of obsession with a prince, a princess, and a happily-ever-after. Those people had not met my mother. Elisabeth Nordgren started her business to plan corporate events for women and gays which "didn't suck"—her words. She expanded to weddings because it was lucrative. While my mother loved bridal gowns and fashion, she coordinated weddings to make people's lives better. She was a fixer. She was a supermodel-turned-fairy-godmother.

I wanted to fix everything. I was keyed into the needs of

those around me. I was perceptive to a fault, an empath. I was fabulous at my job, but it ran me down. I didn't give a shit about bridal gowns. That wasn't my style. I only desired for everyone to leave happy. I was there for the couple and *their* fairy-tale. I faded into the background, making sure everyone around me got the love story of a lifetime.

Worlds collided, however, with the arrival of George and Paul's family. My imagining differed starkly with reality. The smoke and mirrors were bigger than they had been at any celebrity wedding I'd managed. The entire party stayed in a secure location in Chicago. This was two-pronged. One, it took the heat off the Michigan scene. They were less likely to fly drones over the house for a week or run boats in the lake if they were unaware of the details.

We had put out conflicting rumors about what was going on. Lucy, Natalie's personal secretary, and I bonded over planting blind items and such on both sides of the pond. I couldn't wait to meet her in person, but I'd have to. Everyone was camped in the city. The press were sure that the "gay prince nuptials" would take place at a legendary venue. Their top choices were the Ritz-Carlton, the Knickerbocker's Crystal Room, or The Langham. After all, the King and Queen stayed in the Ritz-Carlton. That would make the most sense.

The goal was for the bridal party, groom's family, and siblings to arrive the day *before* the wedding for the rehearsal, have a luncheon, and return to Chicago. They would arrive in planes. They would return the following day for the wedding in cars under the cover of early morning and with lots of secret maneuvering. George and Patrick would receive their guests, start the party, and be wed on their terrace overlooking the lake. Charlotte would play flower girl. The party would continue up the road at the hotel. The amount of security required to pull this off—under wraps—was startling.

It gave me a blank canvas from which to work. An unexpected benefit was my coordination with security officials.

Without everyone present and with their help, vendors could come in and out of the house all day without disturbing a soul. Unfortunately, this also meant that I almost never saw Paul. Our days grew so short. And here I was toiling in Planner Mode, totally avoiding the man I loved most. I hadn't even said a word to his parents or younger sister. We shot texts back and forth but that was all it was. He'd promised me months before that he'd be unable to make much of a fuss about me during this wedding week. It was now clear what he meant.

Paul called as I planned an arrangement for 200 people on the terrace, off the living area. I realized I did so before taking stock of where to put the old people. It was the first contact I'd had from him in twenty-four hours. While I normally found him a bit distracting while I was working, I was all too happy to answer. I missed him.

"Hi, Paul?"

"Hi, darling. How are you? I'm sorry I didn't ring you last night—"

"No, no, it's alright," I answered him. "I missed you but I'm good. I am measuring the tiles in your brother's living room and waiting for Susie to bring me my second large iced coffee of the day."

"Doing the work, I see?"

"It all has to go perfectly, so yes."

"I am sure it *will* go perfectly. Or no one will be the wiser, either way."

"Bingo. At least I can hope. How is everyone?"

"George told everyone last night about the baby," Paul sighed. "Mum cried. It was hard. Lucy's here and I think her mere presence is bothering George. Unfortunately, as you well know, she's crucial to making sure this all goes off at all."

"Correct. I am dying to meet her, meanwhile."

"You will. She's coming over tomorrow with Nat and I. That's why I called you. I am dying to see you. Would you mind terribly if I played errand boy?"

"No." I tried not to be too effusive.

"Good. I will see you then, my love. I will send you details."

My love. That was worse than *darling.* I wasn't used to Paul's sweet terms of endearment. No one called me *my love* before. I hated the fact that it didn't make me want to tell him to fuck off. I was becoming some sort of sweet sap.

"I love you and I miss you," I promised.

"I love and miss you, too," he said. "I wish I could do all sorts of terrible things to you—lovely ones, too."

"Will we get any time together tomorrow?" I asked.

"I dunno. Lucy has been eating ice cream nonstop. So, I suppose we could send the others up to get ice cream and have some quiet time to ourselves."

"Is it ever quiet?"

"Nah. Don't go silent on me," Paul said with a laugh. "I will do my best to engineer it. This is the longest I've gone without you in ages, and I loathe it."

"Don't think about after Labor Day, then—"

"Agreed. I won't."

It was the cliff we refused to acknowledge. I told him I loved him in a sickeningly sweet way and hung up. It was impossible not to love Paul. I adored him. I wanted nothing more than to be *his.* I walked into the dining area and stared at the kitchen door. I looked to the spot where he had stood, shirtless and impolite, and I laughed to myself. I loathed him then.

Now, all I could muster was being a bit of a grump at times when he pushed my buttons by bouncing off the walls in the morning. I was a quiet morning person, but now I loved his spirit. He often lacked self-awareness. Still, I fell for his childlike sense of wonder, his belief that people were inherently good, and his impeccable timing—even if I would complain about it a bit first. I basked in *how* he loved me.

I was wrapped up in those feelings when the phone rang. I hoped it was him. Instead, it was a D.C. number. Was this the press? God, I hoped not. We had been so *painfully* organized.

"Hello. Sanne Holmes-Nordgren here," I said, nervously.

"Yes, Miss Holmes-Nordgren, this is Patrice Louis. I am the Chief of Staff to President Hernandez. Is this a good time to talk?"

I was dumbfounded. In fact, I was sure this was an attempt to get me to speak to the press. It had to be a crank call.

"I'm very sorry. I'm in the middle of planning an event that is rather high-profile. Could you give me your number and extension so I could call you back?"

"Yes, of course. I understand," she agreed.

I scribbled down her number and extension. I googled it. It was legitimate. I called back.

"Apologies," I said after she answered. "I just… I am hosting a very important and secret sort of event at present and—"

"I appreciate your discretion, Miss Holmes-Nordgren. You are running the event for the UK delegation, right?"

Delegation. We were talking in code?"

"Yes. I can say that. It's public knowledge."

"It's something we're aware of, too. We've been coordinating with the King's and Princess of Wales's staff. You were named on all the contracts as the main point of contact. I confirmed that with Lady Ferguson this morning."

I realized Lady Ferguson was Lucy, Countess of Lauderdale, after a moment. God, what was this life I was living?

"Yes, I am the point of contact. I'm lead on this event."

"Great. Well, this is a little ridiculous. And I am sorry I am bothering you. However, our Social Secretary will be retiring in December. We are seeking qualified candidates to take on the position. Your name crossed my desk again this morning. I reached out to a couple of people from Chicago. You seem to have worked with everyone. It's clear you can manage a circus. The President would like someone new, resourceful, connected, and down-to-Earth to take up the reins. I would *love* to set up some time in the next couple of weeks to sit down with you and our Social Secretary. I will warn you that this would be a long process, but we would be so pleased to meet you."

The Chief of Staff was calling me. The *President's* Chief of Staff? To offer me a chance to interview for a dynamite job? I couldn't believe it! I was stunned and worried about saying *anything*.

"I would love to," I said. "I'm booked for the next two weeks but if I could come mid-week the following week, that would be great."

"Love it. Yes, that would be fine. We have a lot of lead time and know that most planners aren't available to meet right now," the woman said.

"Well, thank you Ms. Louis. It's wonderful to hear from you. I'm honored to be considered."

"Of course. It's a hard job but rewarding. We need someone who can handle talent and a crisis. You came with wonderful recommendations from Retired Senator Cahill and Representative Jenkins."

I was surprised Cahill had anything good to say about me after the disaster that was his grandson's wedding. Christ. Although, I did manage a crisis there. And, in the end, they ended up married and happy. It seems that maybe even the Senator was aware that his family was a fuck up.

"Well, that is good to hear," I said as Susie walked in.

"We will be in touch about details. Thank you for your time."

She hung up.

"Who was that? Everything okay? You look like you've seen a ghost," Susie said.

"Uh, that was the President's Chief of Staff. She was wondering if I would be interested in interviewing for White House Social Secretary."

"Holy shit, Sanne! That's amazing!"

"I know. And *terrifying*. They'll fly me out in a few weeks to meet with the current one. What on Earth am I going to wear?"

"You'll figure it out. We'll ask your mother and she'll know what to wear."

"That's true."

"What about Paul?"

That was the question I was ignoring. Paul was all I could think about. And, now, there was even more uncertainty.

"I don't know. We were always planning to do the long-distance thing. D.C. is closer than London."

"But with *that* schedule?"

"It's a lot, I know. A lot to consider," I winced.

she's not the help

. . .

paul

"Dad, we need to chat." I tried to get a word in edgewise with my dad.

It was rehearsal day. We were preparing to fly to Michigan. Sanne would be there. I wanted her to meet my parents. I meant to do this days ago. Of course, my father was always busy with something. Getting a word with him was nearly impossible. The stakes were high. If they arrived and it appeared I *hadn't* told them, Sanne was going to be livid with me. She'd think I was trying to hide her once more. I wasn't. I adored her. I was lovesick and wondering how I would ever leave her without being heartbroken. I had buried my head in the sand over the summer.

He turned away from my Uncle Duncan. "Yes, Paul. What now?"

"Like... alone?"

"We're about to take off. Your sister has already left—"

"I'm aware but I've been chasing you down all week to no avail and if I don't do this until I land—"

I saw mother approaching with champagne. Aunt Rebecca followed.

"Sweetie, why do you look upset?" Mom asked as they sat. "You should sit. We're about to take off."

"Look, I need to say something. Fuck it. I'm dating the wedding planner," I said. "The accomplished American… she's their planner. I think everyone but you all and Kiersten know. She's splendid. I wasn't hiding her. I was insulating her from anything until we knew more."

"You're dating the wedding planner?" Uncle Duncan asked.

"Don't take the piss," I said, annoyed. "Be nice to her. She's lovely. She deserves all the respect in the world—"

"No one here is going to take the piss, darling," my aunt said. "I am sure she *is* lovely. We'll be nice. Duncan is just surprised."

My Uncle chuckled. "Given you're the only one who has dated *up*, I am only surprised you are going to date a normie. Of course, people in glass houses… it's no comment on her."

My parents gave him a nasty look.

Mum said, "Well, that's nice."

Unfussed, Dad said, "Well, thank you for alerting us. I am not sure what the point is—"

"Because I want to introduce you to her, obviously. Also, she's not the help, okay? We're going to treat her well. Natalie went off on her in France and now she's petrified of her. I'd like to avoid that."

"Why did Nat go off on her?" Mum asked.

"It had to do with a stripper, but *nothing* to do with Sanne. It was Gerry's fault."

"Strippergate?" Uncle Duncan asked.

"Yes. You heard?"

"Rita laid into him," Mum said. "We all heard. Sheena was unimpressed."

"Brilliant. Natalie apologised for being bitchy. The damage was done, though. This is all very intimidating to a normie—and an American."

"Honey, if anyone is going to understand, I will. She's in good hands. Your father and I will welcome her."

"Of course. This is… serious?" Dad raised his left eyebrow.

"Yes, Dad. Don't ask me what our plan is. We don't have one. Both of us have been so head down. We intend to keep this going. I love her, alright? She's wonderful."

"Lovely? Wonderful? I am excited to meet her," my aunt said.

"Go sit down," mother beckoned. "We need to leave. Stop fretting about this. Go entertain your grandmother."

I took a seat next to my mother's mother, the former Countess of Dwyfor. She listened to our entire conversation and wanted to know absolutely everything about Sanne. I normally avoided telling my oft-pretentious, meddling grandmother much, but I was in the mood to gush this morning. I supposed worry had turned into relief today. I couldn't say enough about Sanne. She was lovely. I was in love. All I wanted was happiness.

When we arrived, George and Patrick greeted us with a cocktail. The house was transformed for a fabulous luncheon. It was spectacular. I found Sanne in the kitchen dealing with the caterer. She was caught off-guard and not sure what to say. It was always debatable which level of formality she would choose. Today, she seemed all business. She even held a clipboard in her hand. I was keen to shake her formal persona.

"Your Royal Highness, you should not—"

"Stop," I said. "Don't do that. Come, meet my family."

"I've got this," she grumbled. "Can you just wait?"

"You're going to make my parents wait?"

"Would you like me to feed them or not?"

She had a point.

"You just like to keep me waiting."

"No. I like happy clients, Paul."

I left but didn't kiss her. I wanted to *so* badly. Sanne was working. I did not want to put her in a bind with vendors. It would have been unprofessional. I now knew better. Initially, I thought vendors were basically like palace staff. Not so. They were of the same rank as a coordinator even *if* they took delega-tion. I had no idea how to act in the real world. This much was clear.

"Paul, there you are. We want a picture," Patrick said.

"Oh sure, yeah," I agreed, waiting for someone to hand me a camera.

"No, there's a photographer," George said. "Don't be daft, brother. Come on, it's a full-family photo on the terrace. I didn't know where you'd disappeared to."

"We hired a photographer?"

"It was in the run-of-show," Natalie rolled her eyes, practi-cally pulling me onto the terrace. "Your girlfriend doesn't force you to read it?"

"We try to keep work and life separate."

"That's cute," Natalie said.

We crowded for a photo, trying to look relaxed. This was nearly impossible. Mum griped at Dad to loosen up, him protesting that this was already his laid-back look. Kiersten burst into a fit of laughter. I followed. We got the stink-eye from George and Natalie. Finally, we all pulled a photo off—mostly—which didn't scream "an official portrait". As we disassembled, I found Sanne waiting around the area off the patio, talking to Patrick's parents.

Keen to steal her away, I said. "Sanne, can I borrow you?"

"Oh, go on, sweetie," Patrick's adorable mother said.

"If you need anything, just let me know, okay?"

Sanne followed.

"You are very excited. Have you taken your meds?" Sanne asked me, voice low.

It wasn't a judgment, but a reminder.

"Shit. No. I'll go in a minute."

"I will remind you again," Sanne said sweetly.

She sensed my routine was so disrupted that I had forgotten half a dozen times that morning. She was protective.

I brought her to my parents and younger sister, proud to
finally do this the right way.

"Dad, Mum, Kiersten," I said, "this is Sanne Homes-Nord-
gren. She's my girlfriend. Also, the planner."

"Hi," Sanne did her best American attempt at a curtsy. "Nice
to meet you, Your Majesties, Your Royal Highness."

"Oh, don't bother with that," Mum shook her head. "Really,
sweetheart. Not here. This is not a state occasion. It's lovely to
meet you. Just call me Vanna."

Mum extended her hand first. I was grateful there was no
hug involved. Mum could be odd with Americans—unpre-
dictable. Sanne was *not* a hugger.

"Oh… okay. Thanks," Sanne said.

"Robbie, please," my father said. "As my wife explained, not
a formal occasion. We're just the parents of the groom. Well, *one*
of the grooms. Do we have to call them Groom 1 or Groom 2?"

"I think George and Patrick works," Sanne said. She looked
at me in a way that suggested she now knew my father was *also*
socially awkward. Well, at least she knew where I got it from.

"Yes, I suppose so."

"And I'm Kiersten. Nice to meet you. You did such a brilliant
job with this. The sea glass is gorgeous," my sister gushed.

"Oh, thanks. It matched the palette I was given. A local artist
made the favours. In fact, almost everything was done locally.
That was Patrick's whole thing. It was a fun challenge."

Mum smiled. "I love it. It's just beautiful here. I understand
the appeal completely. It will be such a nice day tomorrow."

"I hope so. I'm trying my best," Sanne said. "My team is so
excited. My mother will be on hand to help me tomorrow. Rarely
get to delegate to her but it's all hands on deck."

"Sanne's mothers are friends of George and Patrick," I
explained.

"My mother, Elisabeth, is our president. She runs the place.
But she's trying to slide into retirement, so I got to run the show.
It's been a blast. George and Patrick are the sweetest couple. If I

get a moment, I will introduce you to my sister tomorrow. She was here for setup this morning—"

Sanne looked at her assistant.

"Oh, Susie, hey," I said. "Meet my parents and my sister."

I made introductions as she handed an iced coffee to Sanne.

"So, I don't want to bother you or anything, but Linnea is calling from the hotel. We've got a question about linens, and she wants you to give her an answer," Susie said.

"Ugh. Okay," Sanne looked at me. "Sorry, I gotta go. That means they did *not* get the runners I ordered ages ago. We will sort it out."

"Go, go. It was nice meeting you," my mother said. "I am sure we will get more time to talk?"

Sanne looked doubtful but said, "If all goes to plan, I hope!"

Sanne dashed off to put out the fire.

Kiersten said, "She is too clever for you, Paul."

"Hey!" I chuckled.

"She's a total grown up. In a power suit." Kiersten shook her head "Damn. How did you swing that?"

"Kiersten, be nice," Dad said. "It's good that she's a grown up. She should be."

"I like her. She's sweet. Clearly organised," Mum noted. "I like that for you."

"Is she… Norwegian?" Dad asked.

"Her mother is. She was born there and lived there until about the age she started school," I answered. "So, yes. Half."

"This is Elisabeth Nordgren?" Vanna wondered. "Her mother? *The* Elisabeth? The supermodel?"

"Yes."

"Well, makes sense she's pretty," father said. "She is not at all what I expected. I like her. She seems genuine."

"She is. I'll introduce you to her parents tomorrow. They're guests."

"Great," Mum said.

"Mum, stop looking like that," I groaned.

"What? Like what?"

"Like you're surprised I landed her."

"I am. And I am *happy* for you, sweetheart. She's put together and kind."

"I am surprised you're not all over her," Natalie approached. "He was in France."

"She's at work. I cannot be all over her, Nat. Do you see how busy she is?"

"Totally different than she was in France. She's reminding me of Aunt Rita. She snaps her fingers, and everyone snaps to attention. She and Lucy are getting on like a house on fire. I am surprised you would ever go for a woman in a suit."

"She doesn't always show up in a suit. That's her work outfit. She's a professional, Nat."

"Yes, sometimes she's in a little blue bikini," Natalie teased me.

Father was stern, "Leave her be. She's at work. Don't say things like that. If you were working and Paul brought up Ed's damn deodorant ads, you'd be livid, yeah?"

In a past life, Ed had been a shirtless model in a campaign he abhorred. It never got old bringing it up.

"It's even worse since she's a woman," Kiersten pointed out. "Don't objectify her."

"She's also a very nice girl," Mum said. "Let's be good to her, alright? You frightened her, Nat. Be mindful for Paul's sake."

wedded bliss and coming clean

. . .

sanne

I stood the dance floor's edge, arms crossed, and surveyed what I had done. I wondered how it would feel to plan a White House state dinner. I thought about whether I could pull it off. I knew I could. If I could do this, I could do anything. Linny had done her best job to date with the uplighting. The cake was gorgeous. The flowers were perfection. Everything was top-notch. I couldn't imagine a nicer wedding if I tried. And, despite that, it was relaxed. It was a casual, beachy, family-focused affair. I had done what initially felt would be impossible. I was proud.

Mamma approached with a grin, "You did it, Sanne.".

"I think so, Mamma."

"It looks wonderful. Not that I doubted you. I didn't. You did such a beautiful job with the vendors and the coordination. There were no hitches."

"There was an issue with the linens, but I took care of it. No one noticed—thank God!"

"They are happy. Nothing could have kept them down," she said. "The families are happy, too. George's mother went on and on about how well it worked and how much fun they all have been having. You did well."

"I got a huge tip. I have so much cash, I'm going to have to run to the night deposit box," I scoffed. "Like, in a minute. The Queen is far from stingy."

"She's as sweet as I could have imagined."

I nodded.

"Sanne, this is a big deal. You did a big, beautiful job. Take stock. At your age, I never would have been capable—"

"I know, thanks," I laughed. "You always say that."

"I mean it. You and Linny do such beautiful work. You are so well-organized and prepared. At your age, I was doing coke and parading around in a bikini."

"TMI, Mamma!"

"Well, it's true. I settled down and had two beautiful girls and we could not be prouder of them. Smart, compassionate, dutiful. You are all those things, Sanne. Don't forget it."

"Thanks."

"I'm going to find Marie. Linny is over there with that contractor of hers and Marie looks bored. Time to dance."

Mamma left, spinning Marie around. In her wake, Mom now approached, holding drinks for us.

"You pulled it off, kid."

"I did. And you don't have to tell me. Mamma just hit me in the feels. You know I hate that."

"Ah, it's good. They're so happy. All of them. I have a feeling that if you need a reference, you're about to get a rousing one."

"I might need it," I said.

Mom looked surprised.

"I um… I got a call from the White House."

She laughed.

"No, Mom, really. I got a call from the Chief of Staff. The runaway bride and groom's Senator grandaddy gave me a reference. Inexplicably, he appreciated my handling of a delicate situation. I dunno. That and they've been talking to Lucy and

Vanna's staff who recommended me. They'd never even met me. I think they were being generous—"

"Take the chance. Go, go," mother said.

I shrugged. "I dunno."

I was having a hard time avoiding Paul as he and Kiersten jumped about like drunk idiots. Drunken shenanigans for royals were just like everyone else. George and Natalie had been all over the place. Like Linny and I, where one went, the other followed.

"Ah, that," Mom saw where I stared.

"Yeah. I haven't told him. I agreed to the interview but I hadn't told him and—"

"You aren't married or living together. There is no reason why you must clear things with him. That said, I think it's important for you to tell him."

"Why? So he can leave me?"

"Oh, Sanne, he's not going to do that. He's been staring at you like you're the only thing in the room. I want to tell him off, but I am happy he loves you and I'm feeling protective. I don't want to see you get hurt."

"So, you think he will?"

"No. I don't. You're my babies. I'm going to be a bit Mama Bear about it."

"But should I even let him go on thinking about it? I mean, if I move to D.C.?"

"First of all, you have no idea if you will get this job. I know they'd be stupid *not* to hire you, but you know how that place is. Second, who is to say that if you moved to D.C. anything would be different than if you stayed here?"

I didn't know. That was the thing. It could be the end of us or a new chapter. Either way, I loved him. I loved his stupid, goofy, off-beat self. I wanted Paul in my life. I also knew that waiting for a man to step up and be The One was not for me. If it were meant to be, it would.

"What if he's upset?"

"He's not much of a potential partner then. I think you are underestimating him. His father was telling me that he's coming back to the UK to work. I don't know if you know what that means, but he's not going to have a lot of free time, either. I think it's better for you to have a plan than to wait around missing him. It will work out or it won't. I'd hate for you to put all your eggs in either basket. The way I see it you don't have to."

"I can have my cake and eat it to?"

"You can have both," Mom smiled back at me. "I love you, sweetheart. I know there are no easy choices in life. However, if you are willing to be brave, I know you will make the right ones. I must trust we raised you right. Your work speaks for itself. You are thriving. You're ready for a new challenge—or two."

"You really think it could work?"

"I think they could hire you, yes. I think you will knock their socks off. As for Paul, I have never seen you as relaxed with anyone else. That's saying something, given all of this. You love him. That much is true."

"I have never been so attracted to anyone in my life," I admitted. "Or felt so strongly about anything."

"Well, then, you love him. Make it work. Give it a shot, at least."

I stared at Paul and shook my head. He was gorgeous.

"I gotta run to the bank," I groaned. "I have thousands of dollars in fifties to put in the bank. Why fifties? Who tips in fifties other than the King?"

"I don't think they have hundreds in the UK, if I recall. It makes sense to them. Buy yourself something nice. Don't spend it on anyone but you. Spend it on something downright frivolous, okay?"

"Twist my arm," I laughed.

I left, slammed a shot at the bar since I was off-duty, and grabbed Paul. I was three drinks in, compared to his however many but I felt good.

"I need you to help me run an errand," I said.

He didn't respond at first, just gave me a big kiss. Normally, I would have eyerolled, but it felt so good. We'd barely spoken all day. I was missing this.

"Stay with me tonight," he said. "I'll run an errand if you stay with me."

"Paul—"

"They aren't your clients anymore and they're leaving for their honeymoon in—"

"Forty-five minutes," I finished.

"So, just come back with me. We'll have the house to ourselves, and I can take in every bit of you."

I wanted that.

I sighed, "Fine. I will go back with you and break my own rules. Now, come on."

I led him to the office off the kitchen and grabbed the huge night deposit envelope. I was used to getting cash tips from happy clients, but this was otherworldly. I threw the bag in my purse.

"What are we doing? Meeting the mob? Please say there is a Chicago mob and we are meeting them? Or is it drugs?"

"There is a mob but we aren't meeting them. It's not drugs. Your mother handed me a hell of a tip and it needs to go to the bank."

"Oh, shit. Well done," Paul said while we moseyed through the lobby.

We walked down the street and up the hill. Our bank was a block east.

"So," I said. "You're my muscle. I also wanted to tell you something."

"Please don't break up with me in front of a bank," Paul said as I put the key into the night deposit.

"Are you crazy? No. But like… what would be preferable?"

"I dunno. I don't really want you to break up with me."

"I'm not."

I tossed the wad of cash in and closed the drawer. I turned, walking towards the venue.

"I have a potential job offer—I am in the early stages—and it's in D.C."

"D.C. is closer."

"It's also so far from my family and still far from you. And… it's the White House, so it's not a joke."

"What? How? Tell me about it!"

To my surprise, he was excited.

"It's the job of White House Social Secretary. The President's Chief of Staff called me."

"Well, fuck, that's amazing. You'd be like Lucy on steroids. You could harness all the power of the dignitaries and socialites in D.C."

"That makes it sound much more exciting than most people would think, but sure," I said with a laugh.

"Why do you seem nervous?"

"It's scary. It's not a job with a lot of flexibility. I was worried—"

"I want you to move with me to the UK. That's not practical. It's fucking ridiculous is what it is. But maybe someday you will? Why take a chance and break it off now over a maybe. Maybe I'll move here? Maybe I'll hate working for my Dad? Maybe I'll be like George? I don't know. What I do know is that I love you. And I want to give this a good shot."

His eyes were full of love. Pure, unadulterated love. Paul didn't want to fight. He wasn't angry.

I smiled.

We returned to the party where Gerry pulled Paul away with force. I got myself another drink at the bar in the meantime.

The Queen approached. "Do you all have any plans for next week? I never asked."

"We're trying to relax," I answered. "It's going to be hard. I guess we'd both like to pretend what is happening isn't."

My drink appeared. A G&T was my wedding go-to. She grabbed a glass of champagne.

"I don't want to say too much. I don't know you, Sanne. I feel like I do, though. Maybe that's just what we have in common talking? I do know my son. He's a born romantic like his father. He also needs someone steady to rein him in."

"He's plenty steady," I said. "When he feels needed and important. He likes to have a job. He's very compassionate and dedicated. He would kill for any of you."

"I know," Vanna said. "God, you're so sweet. I really am sad we did not get to spend much time together. You should come and visit soon. Stay with us. Really let us get to know you."

It was an unexpected and kind offer. I had not anticipated that they would *like* me, let alone want to *know* me.

"You look frightened—"

"No, no. Just surprised. You're really kind, Your Majesty. I expected you to be like, 'it's a summer fling and best of luck.' Because, to be honest, I thought it was until I began considering the end of summer. I loved him, but I feared he'd break my heart. God, I don't know why I just said that—"

"People tell me things. I guess I have one of those faces or something. Well, I get it. Paul's father and I got together in June and were engaged within a year. I left in September, and we were both heartbroken over it. He confessed his love for me—accidentally—over the phone. Anyhow, I was supposed to stay here, but by October I moved to the UK forever. By May, I moved into Robbie's place. Life happens fast. Sometimes, it is worth taking the chance and saying, 'we don't know how it will work, we just hope it will.' That's what George did. And now, look at how happy he is."

I smiled, looking at the crowd.

"Yeah, I hope you're right," I said. "We do hope it will."

leaving on a jet plane

. . .

paul

Sanne and I spent the next five days alone in George and Patrick's house. We lounged on deck and in the sand. We spent an ungodly amount of time in bed. We ate loads of takeout, burgers, and drank too much beer. Thankfully, Sanne spent most time either in minimal or *no* clothing, allowing me to soak up a few more hours with her.

Then, it was our last night. Gone was the sand. Gone was the sound of the waves. We wound up in Sanne's Chicago flat listening only to emergency vehicles and the air conditioner. Still, I was with her. It was the last night I would fall asleep next to her. Tomorrow, it would be the last morning I saw her face. It was difficult. I didn't know much other than I planned to see her in Oslo after a month.

We sat on her couch eating tacos, enjoying the last hours we'd have before I boarded a plane and returned to my normal life. Or, rather, my new normal.

"I just want to say," Sanne said. "The last few days have been some of my best. And not just because I can be lazy."

"Oh?" I asked.

"I have loved the normalcy. We finally had some time to just *be*. And it made me love you more. I didn't run away screaming. I want more of it—a lot more."

"I'll come back for Thanksgiving," Paul insisted. "We can just be normal again. Unless, you're in D.C. or you just don't want me—"

She shook her head.

Sanne put her taco down and kissed me. "I love you. I want you here. It doesn't matter where I'm at. And, anyway, where I am, you are welcome."

I agreed. "Same. I mean that, Sanne."

"I know. Your Mum says she wants to get to know me. Maybe I could come in December or early November? Or, maybe I could come for a little bit before you come back? We could fly back together?"

"I'd like that," I said. "But I'd like any excuse to see you."

"Let me finish my taco before we dive back into this. You're making me want to throw everything to the wayside."

"I can let you finish your taco. Important things first."

"I need sustenance to keep up with you."

She finished and we did not make it two feet, going at it on the couch like desperate teenagers finally left alone by parents. There was nothing delicate or calm about it. It was messy in the best of ways. We'd had too much tequila. I'd like to say that was it and we got our acts together, but we did not. We took a shower only to wash and dive back into bed.

It was unplanned. I pulled her in to kiss her neck when she rocked into me and I couldn't help myself. I threw her on the bed, ripping off her shorts and knickers. I proceeded to go down on her one last time. She climbed on top of me until we both were satisfied, exhausted, and almost forlorn. It was a mix of emotions.

"I don't want to go," I confessed.

Sanne cupped my cheek. "I don't really want you to, but you know you can't stay."

I kissed her again, slowly, taking her in. I brushed my hands through her silky hair. I'd miss her soft amber-hued locks and the way her skin felt against mine. It was so soft.

"You should go," she said.

I looked at my phone. The car was already downstairs with my luggage. *Ah, the motorcade! Great fun.*

I pulled my trousers on. "I love you, Sanne. I promise I will see you again soon."

She looked up from the bed. Her face was sad, but she was trying to smile. She was trying so hard to act like this was all okay and she didn't mind. She did, though. I bent down to kiss her again.

"I love you," Sanne said. "I hate that I love you because it makes my life so complicated. I also love that I love you because I didn't see it coming and you make me laugh—a lot."

I was choked up. "You make me laugh, too, if only because you infuriate me in the best of ways."

She left the bed, pulled on a dressing gown and padded to the door as I rolled my carryon. I opened the door, staring. It killed me to leave.

"Don't leave forever, okay?" Sanne asked.

"I won't. I will be back. You are not rid of me yet, my love."

She smiled, tears welling, gave me a last kiss, and I departed. By the time I was on the lift, I wiped tears. God, she hit me in the feels in a way I hadn't expected. I boarded my flight back and settled in, feeling a strange bit of homesickness. Strangely, the time spent in the States was calming. I found my genuine self. I watched George be his most George and saw Patrick be his most Patrick. I had grown. I would miss that little lakeside town with its beachy-hued houses, its friendly shops, and all the gluttonous food on offer.

Now, all I could hope was that I hadn't lost all sense of self.

Or, really, that I wasn't about to lose the light in my eyes again. After landing, I was whisked to Windsor. It was early, I hadn't slept well, and I wished I could lay in bed listening to Sanne's little happy groans as she nodded off. I still smelled like her perfume. It felt good somehow, like I hadn't lost her. I was taken to my parents' dining room for breakfast. They were happy to see me.

"How are you?" Mum asked. "You look exhausted."

"I'm alright. Knackered."

Dad asked, "You miss her?"

I nodded.

"You'll see her again," mother assured. "She seems like a very nice girl."

"I love her. She's going to be busy, but I will see her. I promised her, anyway," I said.

Father spoke, "I remember when your mum left. I was heartbroken."

"You learned about your mum's cancer diagnosis the same day, though," Mum pointed out.

"I did. I still would have been a mess, either way."

"I missed you. The minute I got back. Which is why I practically got on a plane and came right back to you."

"Did you know that you'd see her again?" I asked.

"Mum was certain of it. She was clear that we'd see one another again. I worried she'd run off and never return. I am sure that Sanne probably finds herself a bit nervous."

"She works a lot, Dad. I just hope—"

"I will make sure that you have time to see her. I allow Natalie time off to see Ed. I took time to see your mother. My schedule is not set to completely run me into the ground. Family comes first. I won't say you cannot see her. What I will say is you need to be focused on work if you are here."

"Of course."

Father sighed. "I suspect that things are about to get more

chaotic, as well. Full disclosure. Ed was basically thrust onto our hunting trip."

He spoke as if suspecting I would know what it meant.

"Calm down. You didn't see this coming?" Mum rolled her eyes.

"See what?" I was so confused.

"Natalie will not be on the hunting trip despite her many protests. Every year with her."

"It's a bit sexist, Dad"

"Every year she wants to come along," Mum shook her head. "And you tell her no."

"Because it's the *one* week a year, it's just the men of the family."

"That's not it at all, Dad."

"Then what is it?"

"She can outshoot the entire party and you don't like being embarrassed."

I sat back and crossed my arms. I was right. Father glared as mother burst into laughter. *Mission accomplished.*

"The point is that Ed has invited himself along since he's in with Duncan now."

"He's not in with Duncan. He is simply allowed to come along. It's not just him It's all of you. Duncan wanted to include him since you haven't made much of an effort."

"We don't have much in common. I'm not known to take my shirt off and take photos."

"Thank God," I groaned. "Dad, what the fuck does this have to do with anything? So, Ed wants to come with? He just spent the week with us like part of the family. He's a good guy. He loves Nat. He's good for her."

"He's divorced and half-Catholic. His mother is proudly Irish. It's something else."

Mum was at her wit's end from prior rowing. "You will say yes and let her be happy, Robert! You are being so annoying."

"I don't dislike him. But he's not my son. I have no intention—"

"Dad, what is it that Ed coming along represents in the story of our lives?"

"It's not obvious?"

"No, Dad."

"Well, he's about to propose to your sister. This is him trying to buddy up to me so I will grant my consent."

"Fucking hell, Dad. That's good! Good for them. Don't be so cunty."

"Is it? Because I think that with a royal wedding comes more work your sister cannot do. She's a bride. Brides are busy with wedding things."

"You think that Natalie will be bride-y?" I snickered.

"Perhaps."

"I think she is more apt to care about organising the flyover than she is a floofy dress or flowers, Dad," I said.

"I agree," mother nodded. "Sweetheart, she will be fine. But your father isn't wrong, either, Paul. There will be more work to go around. There will be more visibility. Buckle up and prepare to work hard. Prepare to help Ed integrate."

"I'll say yes, I assume, if that is what she wants. However, I will tease out whether he is serious or not."

"Dad, he loves her. She loves him. More than you could even know, okay? Just let him do the thing."

"We want the best for your sister."

"We all want the best for Natalie," Mum said. "You and I. All of us. However, Robert, torturing Ed will only alienate him. Don't be your mother."

"I promise not to be Mum."

"Good, then do it."

Dad asked, "I don't suppose Sanne does British weddings?"

"I am not even sure she will be doing weddings much longer," I admitted. "She might be working for the President— managing their engagements. As a social secretary."

My parents stared down the table at me.

"Go ahead and say it," I sighed. "I know she is too good for me. She's amazing. I know that."

"She is good for you," mother said, voice sweet and genuine as ever. "She is a bright, lovely person from what I can tell. You deserve someone like that."

the big interview

. . .

sanne

The day of my big interview, I arrived at the gated staff entrance of The Executive Residence, or just The Residence, which is what people called The White House. Well, it's what people who spoke to me had been saying. I was trying to fit in and feel less like a flat-out Midwesterner. I had a lot of big-fish-small-pond energy coming into this.

I wanted to be confident but spent the whole time feeling less-than. At least I looked good. My mother spared no expense in getting me a proper suit and had sent me a set of Louboutin's as a "go get 'em, girl" gift. I looked like a million bucks. I felt like maybe eighty.

"Yes, Sanne Holmes-Nordgren," I reported to the guard. He asked me to spell my last name, "That's N-O-R-D-G-R-E-N."

He nodded. "For Chief Louis?"

"Correct. Thanks."

He called someone and had them lead me in.

"I'm Jen," the young woman said. "I'm an assistant to the Chief. Glad to meet you, Ms. Nordgren."

She dropped Holmes. Still, I preferred Nordgren. In circles

like this, I always felt more cosmopolitan. I knew it would hurt Mom's feelings to say that but it was true. Americans found my somehow-impossible-to-spell last name to be the more fabulous one. Men of a certain age always knew how to spell it. I tried not to read too much into it. Just like I tried not to know why King Robert looked nervous about knowing *of* my mother. I always prayed such men weren't about to tell me that my mother was the first person they ever jerked it to. I'd gotten that. It was so inappropriate.

Jen knocked on the door, "Patty, Ms. Nordgren is here for you."

"Oh, please, let her in," the woman on the other side replied.

Jen escorted me inside. Patrice Louis was a short and somewhat stout woman I would recognize anywhere. She was dressed in her signature look–a fun, printed dress. She wasn't stodgy or uptight. She kept life a bit light. The President must have appreciated that. She was very different from the old men who came before her. I was overly excited to meet her but kept my fangirling to an absolute minimum.

"Ms. Nordgren, so great to have you. Thanks for coming out." Patty shook my hand.

"Oh, so glad to be here," I replied. "I am over-the-moon to get the chance."

Ah, there it was. Paul's vernacular invaded my brain.

"Jen, can you grab us something to drink? I'd take a coffee. You?" Patty asked.

I responded, "Coffee is fine, thank you."

"You're welcome," Jen said.

"Sit, sit."

Patty sat at her office table. I sat across from her, placing my beloved portfolio down.

"So, Northwestern for your undergrad, a Kelley MBA, and you work for a large events company? Well, *the* planning company in the upper-Midwest."

"Well, the Great Lakes Region for sure," I said. "Mostly

Chicagoland and southwestern Michigan. Sometimes, southern Wisconsin but I'm not usually handling those. The events there are generally smaller."

"So, you run the more prestige ones?"

"I tend to. I love chaos and herding cats. I thrive on it. But I treat every event with the same degree of respect. My favorite part of the job is the clients and relationship-building. The goal is to please them and make them have the best, least-stressful day on one of the most-stressful days of their lives."

"And how long have you been working in the business?" she asked.

"About ten years. It's a family-business, full disclosure. I started as an assistant in high school, worked all through college, worked the summers in graduate school, and then promoted to a junior planner and senior planner soon after. My mother and I tag-team now. We're the two senior-most staff in the company."

"You were working in college?"

"I ran events all through summer. I didn't have a lot of a social life, if we're being honest. But I'm pretty married to the job."

"Good, good. Are weddings your favorite?"

"I like all events. Weddings are fun, but I love crisis management and relationship-building, like I said. It doesn't matter what the goal is."

Patty nodded as the assistant returned. Jen sat our drinks on the table and left, closing the door.

"This is a whole new world," Patty said. "But what we need is someone who can manage talent and neurotic people. How do you feel about criticism—giving it and taking it?"

"I am a bit blunt. My mother is Norwegian and since she basically trained us all, I suppose I am most comfortable with a less-hierarchical style where respectful criticism is valued and given pretty freely. It is important with a staff to let them feel like you are communicating. A friend called this the importance of having a first officer. My junior planner who is my go-to will always remind me if I mishear or say something off. She will call me out if I do not follow a checklist."

"I like that analogy. Checklists are crucial here. And being open to criticism is essential. It is something that Elaine thrives on. Every President or cabinet member is different is different. Every head of state is unique. Culturally, that can be a challenge. Of course, I think you know something about that now?"

"I do," I agreed. "I coordinated with the Norwegians and Belgians along with the Brits on this one. You all did, too. Security is crucial. I learned a lot. I am used to discretion and talent, as you say, being a challenge. But I just let it roll off. These are busy, opinionated people. They are all a little high strung and stressed. I get used to people shouting at me, quite frankly, in times of stress."

"What is the most complicated situation you have ever dealt with?"

"I had a runaway bride and a verbally abusive mother-in-law," I replied.

"Ouch. How did you handle it?"

"The couple are my clients. I de-escalated the situation best I could there. In the end, the groom ran off on a honeymoon with the bride and I arranged their civil ceremony a week after they returned free of charge. Because, again, I love my job and they had spent a year of their lives with me planning. I see things through even if I must put in some extra hours. The family has de-escalated, too. Honestly, one of them gave you a reference I was not expecting. We did handle it. I cannot take full credit. I have a wonderful staff who managed the vendors, got the payments, and made sure guests could get back to their cars on the busses we had hired."

"That's a lot."

"It's a lot but we have a disaster plan. I am sure that you all do, too. Checklists and plans are essential."

"I would agree. You must. And not just with us. You're talking embassies, the Secret Service, the FBI—everyone. It is intense. I have learned so much from Elaine. By the way, she's going to love you."

I smiled a bit.

"We need someone who can handle the heat. She is going to have the most weight in finding this replacement. She is a national treasure here."

I smiled and nodded. "That's what I have heard. It is a tough job. I know I am young, but I promise you I have the experience to be good at this. It has always been my dream to work in this place, believe it or not. I am sure you get that a lot. But really, it is so wonderful to get a shot at it."

"Great. It's challenging but you seem to have come prepared and you're being honest. I need that in any member of staff."

"Of course. Can I ask a question?"

"Certainly!"

"What would the timeline be like?"

"You would probably start around Christmas. That is a very busy time. Elaine plans to train her replacement as a trial-by-fire. Sorry for that but it's the best way to get a feel for where everything is. She will have you run a couple of events with her help. If it works, you will start in January. We won't be offering this to more than one finalist. However, we want to give you an honest appreciation for what you would be doing. Thus, you'd be hired in at an assistant rate. The job pays much better at her rate. We can talk compensation and expectations if you get an offer."

I nodded. I fully expected to take a pay cut. I didn't want to, but I knew I would make a great deal from the sale of my Chicago apartment and could live spartan for a bit. It wasn't about the money. It was about the experience. This was a dream job.

"That sounds like a really solid plan for both the applicant and for the social secretary."

"It is. Elaine wants to retire first of the year, but her retirement date is dependent on finding the right person."

I nodded at that.

"You'll meet her tomorrow. She's busy running an even for Mrs. Hernandez. The First Lady will meet with you this afternoon, as well. She's very excited to chat. She knows your mothers, I guess."

"My Mom, yes. She only has great things to say about her. They knew one another from a board they were both on."

"Great. That's a small world thing, isn't it?"

"I nodded.

"Let me give you a tour," Patty said.

I followed Patty through the entirety of the offices off the side of The Residence. I met her assistants, and other staff I'd work with. We went over to The Residence to meet the executive chef and kitchen staff. It was fabulous. I met the First Lady for lunch. That was the chance of a lifetime. She reminded me of Paul's mother—expertly-mannered, generous, and kind. I figured if I had to work with her every day, I would be okay.

I left the meetings hopeful. I really wanted this job. Part of me was sad. I had almost wanted to leave unhappy and dissatisfied. I loved Paul. I wanted to see more of Paul. This job would be less-flexible than my current job. However, it was the chance of a lifetime. I had to take it if it was offered.

Paul called me later. I answered, unsure what to say. Hearing his voice brought a smile to my face.

"So, how was it?" he asked.

"It was nice. Everyone was so nice and excited to meet me. The First Lady is so kind. I would love to work for her. Reminds me of your mum. She's so generous and pretty. Just a real sweetheart. The Chief of Staff seems like a hoot. Overall, a nice time. Even if they don't pick me, it was fun."

"I'm so happy for you, Sanne," Paul said.

"It's late there?"

"It's midnight, yeah," Paul laughed.

"What are you up to?"

"Listening to Dad whinge about Ed. We're going shooting. Ed doesn't shoot. He's only along for the ride because he's trying to get in Dad's good graces. It's a long story. Ed will prevail. I'm also getting fitted for new suits and dealing with staff. Lucy is helping for now. She's trying to hire me some people. I wish you were here for a dozen reasons but I think you could help me choose them. And, anyhow, she's going on leave in a minute. She's going to be gone for *months*. So, of course, Nat is having a mental breakdown."

"Sounds like things are good," I said with a chuckle.

"Just a *bit* of a pickle. That's British for fucked up completely."

"I know, Paul."

"I'll see you in a bit. That's what I'm living for right now," Paul admitted. "I think once I get started, I will like the job. The leadup is sort of dreadful. I wish George would have taught me what the fuck I am doing."

"You'll get it. Don't they like train you? Is there a prince finishing school?"

"I'm the only prince of this generation standing, so no. I wish! I will go out with my Uncle Duncan. He promised to train me up. He's also known for off-the-cuff statements and adorable gaffes. I would just be offensive if I tried his style. So, who knows what I will do."

"You can be really charming, baby," I reminded him. "So charming. But you have to keep your foot out of your mouth and take your medication so you can focus."

"That's alright. Lucy is like a mum. She reminds me. Heaven help us when she leaves."

"She's the glue?"

"She really is," Paul sighed. "Much like I suspect you are, my love. Or, I feel you are. Can't you just move here? I am not serious but I wish it were true."

"Paul, if I take this job, I start in December. It won't be easier. Are you sure—"

"I will wear you down and get you back here one way or the

other," Paul said. "It's a joke, but… it's not. I am not concerned. We will find a way, alright?"

"Okay," I agreed.

"This isn't fleeting for me. I'm also not going to ask you to give up on an amazing opportunity like this. I will never hold you back, Sanne, even if that makes things more complicated in the interim. You are so precious to me."

It was the sweetest thing a man ever said to me. How could I have loved Paul more? He was everything I needed–supportive, not a possessive jerk, and his praise for me was effusive. He loved me in the sweetest, most adorable way a partner could. I hoped he was right. I wanted it to work.

"I love you so much, Paul," I said. "I wish I could kiss you. I wish you could just hug me and make me feel less topsy-turvy. I trust you are right."

"I'll give you a hug in a couple weeks," Paul promised. "And life will always be topsy-turvy. You'll manage."

guns, girls, and gripes

...

paul

Sometimes, princehood was a joke. Other times, I found myself excited about making people happy. I was a people-pleaser. When an event went well, it made me more confident. However, I always had imposter syndrome. I worried everyone would find out that I was a waste of space.

When we left on our shooting holiday at the end of September, I had a few engagements under my belt. It was a confidence boost. I hired a good assistant. He worked well with Mum's staff and Lucy. I hoped he would guide me. I compared two strong candidates and went with my gut. I asked Sanne what she thought and she agreed. I felt a bit more confident with her seal of approval. She was a manager and knew how to hire staff. I was a babe in the woods.

My late grandfather adored this shooting weekend. Uncle Duncan and dad kept it going. He always took George and myself since the start of adolescence. I remembered the sheer excitement of being invited the first time. I felt like a man. It was a coming-of-age thing. I got to drink a beer—courtesy of Uncle Duncan who was the *cool* twin—and shoot a rifle. I was not at all a man's-man. I probably never *would* be. That was more George, ironically. I didn't care much for sport. Dad never was sure where to put me. We struggled to bond sometimes. I was much closer to my mum. However, on this trip I felt included.

This year would be fun, but maybe not in the best of ways. George attended for the first time in two years. Patrick was home playing football. They'd only gotten the by-week to take a short honeymoon before returning to Chicago as I left. We were ships passing in the night. I was relieved to have George along as a buffer with Dad.

However, George's behaviour might be bad. We didn't know. Winston's stepfather, Bruno, always came. This year, with both his stepsons This wasn't new, but there was the George-Winston factor to consider. George was downright *nice* to Lucy at the wedding and had not picked a fight, but I knew that the issue with losing the baby had hurt. I knew George still harboured resentment for Winston. Moreover, he was still cross with Gerry over Strippergate. The weekend would either end with everyone bonding or with everyone fighting.

I hoped that a desire to integrate Ed would unite George, Winston, and I. Known as Project Pants Model, we agreed to help Ed impress Dad. Ed's own father, a former cabinet minister, referred to him The Pants Model ever since the infamous deodorant campaign. Natalie, being the embarrassing and wild person she was, never let it go. Ed loathed Natalie pointing out billboards or joking. That made her do it more. He had been trying *so* hard to distance himself from that image for Natalie's sake though both his father and mine still took the piss.

Ed was perfect for Natalie in most ways. He was kind. He respected that she had an important job, but didn't find it intimidating. He tempered her in important ways. He was well-spoken and worked as a tv presenter in retirement, covering American swimming meets. Overall, he was well-suited for the job and for Natalie. However, his mother was born in Northern Ireland and had been an outspoken nationalist like her ancestors. Ed also had a marriage fail after only a couple of years. He'd since taken things slow and learned a few things. Still, the idea of a divorced person marrying the future Head of State wasn't ideal in father's eyes.

I believed mum when she'd said Dad would get over it. Still, if I knew Dad, he'd whinge about it first. Which he did. He whinged all the way north. George and Ed drove by themselves to Sandringham. I rode with Dad and Uncle Duncan. All Dad did was whinge about Ed being a wuss who didn't want to shoot a rifle.

"Dad, I am not going to go out and kill anything either," I pointed out. "Would you desert me? He just wants to get to know you. Natalie sees this as an important opportunity. Also, you've made no effort to this point. He thinks you hate him."

"Hmmm… is history repeating itself, Robert?" Uncle Duncan asked.

"No. History is not repeating itself. I am not saying now. I am stating that I have *concerns*."

"So did Mum about Vanora and how did that shake out? She is the most beloved member of the family and one of the most beloved queens in British history."

Father knew he was backed against a wall. He was terribly stubborn and did not like to be told what to do.

"It's been a short period—"

"You got engaged to Vanna less than a year after you met her —let alone dated her. Come on now, Robert!"

"Yeah, Dad, they've been together for more than a year. Closer to a year and a half."

"They are also older and wiser than we both were when we married our wives. Note, as well, that we are both still married. And Rebecca, despite being torn apart in the press for being an unwed mother and commoner, is also quite beloved. We haven't stumbled. That is arguably worse in the eyes of the press than being divorced and without children."

"Bex is a gem of a human," father said. "Lovely as could be.

As is Nira. Nira was too adorable to say no to. Rebecca's parents were good, middle-class English people who loved one another very much. Ed's parents are terribly unusual, his mother is a horrid gossip, and—"

"Mum called Hannah a horrid social climber and suspected that Ralph was out of his depth. Despite Hannah being a bit of a pill at times, you managed with Vanna, yes?"

"Dad, c'mon. It's a fucking nothingburger."

"A nothingburger it is not. God, you sound so American."

He said it with disdain but I could only laugh.

"Yes, you loathe that, don't you?" Duncan asked. "You know, brother, it is so trying to watch you comport yourself into knots over Ed. You know you will say yes and he will make an excellent consort. He wants children. They are mad for one another."

"They are insufferable in the best way, Dad."

"You want her happy, don't you?"

"You sound like my wife."

"Who is usually right, brother. And who you take advice from willingly. Don't be like Mum and start a war to rage on for ten years."

"I suppose you all will win out in the end. However, this is the person who will essentially raise my grandchildren—"

"He is great with kids," I insisted. "He's lovely with Charlotte. Natalie loathes babies. I think you have a good shot at actually *having* grandchildren sometime in this century if they end up together. She needs someone a bit broody and older. He's both."

"The boy makes a good point, Robert."

Father gave an exasperated sigh as we pulled into the drive. Here we were—finally. I could not *wait* to leave this vehicle. Inside, we surprisingly found George in good spirits, joking with Ed about something while Winston tended the fire. Gerry was on his phone, walking the halls, panicking about something. All was strangely fine.

"What is he on about?" Duncan asked Bruno of Gerry.

Winston laughed and shook his head.

"Sheena is in some sort of way," Bruno replied. "She seems to be in a panic."

"Over what now?" my father asked. "Is this going to ruin our weekend?"

"Let's hope not. I sent Lucy to console her over something. I won't get into it," Winston said. "But Lucy will *hopefully* talk her off of the ledge. Natalie did not."

"No, Natalie pulled a Natalie and proceeded to tell her to stop bothering everyone. That was... less-than-diplomatic." Gerry looked cross.

"Natalie struggles with women," father said. "Thank God Lucy handles her directness appropriately."

"Sanne is still scared of her," I said.

"I find that silly. Sanne is very direct. More diplomatic, though," George admitted.

"Fucking hell. If your wife cannot salvage this, I have to go home," Gerry said. "Or I will ruin it for the lot of you."

"What now? Did she buy the wrong shoes?" George asked. "I don't know how you put up with it."

"Let's not go down the 'I have no girl problems' route, shall we? You have your own issues just like the rest of us," I said.

Sometimes I reminded George not to be a knob. He could get all high-and-mighty about it. He and Patrick had their own spats like the rest of us.

George glared.

"No, actually. My wife is pregnant and freaking out because this wasn't what we planned," Gerry grumbled. "This was absolutely *not* what she wanted and she's losing her mind over it."

"Even when it's planned, they lose their minds," Duncan said. "This is how it goes. Should I congratulate you or—"

"Yes. I mean, it's not the timeline we would have preferred, but we're having the baby."

"Congrats," I said, feeling an unexpected pang of jealousy.

Again, it made no sense. But, as Sanne reminded me, it didn't have to.

"Thanks, mate. I hope Lucy talks her down."

"If *anyone* can talk her down, it's Lucy," I assured him.

Winston merely nodded.

"Plus they can bond over all of that nonsense," George said.

"It's not nonsense," Winston said, annoyed. "It's literally carrying around another human being in your body. Sheena wasn't interested in doing it yet. Let's give her a bit of credit. It's not a fun experience."

"She's been dreadfully ill for the past week." Gerry shook his head.

"It's a dreadful experience. I don't recommend it," father said.

"As if you would know, Dad!" I laughed. "Mum did all the work."

"Yes, give credit where it is due. We did nothing," Bruno said.

Duncan sat a bottle of whisky down. "Putting up with them is not always pleasant. I am not judging them. I would not like to birth a human or carry one around for months. Sounds horrid. However, dealing with them is… unpleasant. Hormones. Never mention it, of course. That was Dad's advice, and I will give you the same, boys."

Winston, satisfied with the fire, took a seat, "It's too late for Gerry. I explicitly said not to mention it."

"Your wife is the calm one," Gerry said. "I should certainly have listened better. It set mine off and I got a tongue lashing and the couch."

"Oof," my father groaned.

"I think you got off easy. If I mentioned hormones to Nat, I'd be grovelling for a week," Ed said.

Duncan chuckled. "Natalie is like her dear mother, then. Get good at it. Robbie knows a bit about it."

Dad glared.

"Look, she's just *particular* and wants to be right. If you make it *her* idea, all is well," George offered up. "That's the way to criticise Natalie without setting her off. However, hormones is a word you should strike from your own vocabulary with any woman—even your mums and sisters."

"Why *does* that bother them?" I asked.

"Look at the word hysteria," Ed answered. "And consider that. I mean, it's misogyny at the end of the day. I agree pregnancy does not seem like a cakewalk. Grant poor Sheena a bit of grace. I don't feel right taking the piss about it, George."

"Oh, he's being a good boy, then?" George shook his head. "Are you *always* so well-behaved?"

"My father is a scoundrel who would say such things and get slapped on the hand by my mother," Ed replied. "Having a mother quite as headstrong as mine has perhaps made me a little more sympathetic or understanding. She had to fight so hard to be taken seriously at her job. She's a brilliant consultant. I don't pretend to know how hard that is. Also, most of my friends are women, so… I guess I am just a bit more sensitive."

"It's good to avoid, yes," Robbie said.

"Well, I am sure you could relate?" Ed asked.

"No, not really. My mother's internal misogyny was hard to beat—especially when it came to how Vanora and I raised the children. She saw me changing nappies and doing carpool and deemed it a moral failing. She saw Vanora as some sort of over-involved harpy. I mean, she nursed Paul two years and—"

"Dad, fucking stop!"

George roared with laughter.

"You were like Velcro for years, Paul. I am going to say it. My point is that she didn't approve of our parenting. I think our father was probably the driving force in us being involved. He was a very good father, you see. An unusually good one for his time. They never hit us. He was always a sweet, caring person. So, if anything, I got that side from him."

"Me as well, but I'm just a sap deep down," Duncan admitted.

"Well, my father reacted strongly to the implication that a husband would change nappies, so I think you know how mine is," Ed said.

"And that came up how?" Dad's curiosity piqued.

"Oh, well, my mother demanded to know if Natalie *wanted* children. Of course, it's obvious she wants them but also *has* to have them. I explained we *both* want them. Dad asked me if I could handle that because it's about delegation, obviously. Sure, that doesn't really bother me. I said there was no way Natalie would tolerate anyone slacking in that regard—nor could she."

"Natalie would let you know, too," George said. "You put up with her. You are unique."

"She's not a drill sergeant most of the time. She's quite sweet when you get down to it. However, I understand that the job dictates a certain level of authority and delegation. I honestly do *not* mind. I got to play household manager and sole bringer-of-happiness once. I have no intention of being that guy again. That's how you fail at marriage, really. You cannot be everything to someone. I don't have Natalie's bravery or ambition. Perhaps, you all see that as a failing, but I'm old enough to admit it."

I was surprised by Ed's candour. He put it all out there.

"I, personally, feel the same," I said. "I don't think I knew that until Sanne, but I rather like *not* being the one who is helming things. I find it kind of hot, actually. Sorry, Dad, but that sounds fucking exhausting."

"I rather like it," George shrugged. "I suppose that is where we differ. Ironically, I now play professional House Husband. But, really, I still make most major decisions. Pat just delegates it."

"That sounds fucking tiring," I said.

"It's okay to want different things," Uncle Duncan said. "Do not feel less-than. Just be happy you know what you want. Half of life is spent knowing that. I found it early with Rebecca. She had her life together."

"She did by then," father said. "As did Vanna by the time I married her. I really didn't. We grew up together. It was fine."

"I just took a lot longer," Ed chuckled. "But until I retired, I didn't think about my own personal life a lot. Having to take a year off before I could even manage to swim again was a blessing in disguise. I couldn't ignore everything and focus on sport. I had to do a post-mortem. I'm very happy with Natalie despite the press and all that nonsense. That was the hardest part. She's wonderful. I admire her now."

My father looked genuinely surprised.

"Well, she is an ace," Duncan chuckled. "Easily the best airman I have ever flown with. And she's a great co-pilot, too. You'll never wonder where you stand. She will always set you right."

Dad nodded, "That's all true."

I admired Sanne most. I shared in Ed's sentiments. I thought I had loved before, but it seemed childish. That had been fun. Perhaps, it was the wake-up call which forced me to grow a bit and decide what I wanted in life. Now, all I wanted was to get back to Sanne—some way, somehow. She was the one I wanted to spend every day with. While glad for the happily ever after Ed and Natalie got, I wanted the same. Suddenly, it felt in reach. I just had to figure out how to make it work.

the call

. . .

sanne

I walked into the room where Paul unpacked at my mothers' house outside Oslo. I shut the door and locked it.

"What do you think you are up to?" Paul asked.

"They are cooking. We have like thirty minutes to get down to business. I haven't seen you in weeks and I am not wasting even a minute with you."

Paul smiled and dropped what he was doing. He jumped on me, pushing me onto the bed. He kissed me, making my heart race. We didn't tear off our clothing immediately. Instead, he stopped and stared at me in the most loving way. I beamed. I couldn't resist smiling. I missed him so much. I'd been worried about work, closing out the last of the big fall weddings, and worrying about my job prospects. I couldn't shake my desire to see Paul. He was forever.

Paul kissed me again, his lips barely grazing mine at first. It was like he savored it. I felt myself melt. He kissed my neck. I moaned and realized I needed to be quieter. Paul pulled back and disrobed. I threw my clothes off. Again, though, we didn't claw at one another. This was tender. Perhaps, we were both feeling out the situation? Maybe we were just so in love we wanted to take in every moment. Either way, I loved watching everything he did and feeling every touch. I was completely wrapped up in him.

"I love you," I gasped after the first climax. "I love you so, so much."

"I love you, too." His smile said it all.

Oh, he loved me so much. He loved me like no one else.

As we parted, we gazed silent at one another. We lay, staring and breathing again. Finally, Paul rolled onto his side and brushed my cheek lovingly.

"You are the most perfect thing."

He kissed me longingly. I wanted to call him out on how sappy he was being. However, I liked it. I, to this day, will deny that I like this sort of thing. It just runs in opposition to everything I espouse. However, I loved it at that moment.

"I am far from perfect," I protested.

"Take a bloody compliment for once, Sanne."

I was so wrapped up and at peace in his arms. I floated on his love for me. Paul did the impossible. He made me feel like jelly. And rather than resist it, I longed for it. I missed it. I craved this attention and love. I didn't even know who I was. And, as much as I wanted to say I needed it to stop, I didn't. I needed more.

"I never want you to leave," I gasped, astonished by my admission.

Paul stared at me, surprised.

"Sorry."

I immediately sat up, nervous. Paul pulled me down.

"Why on *Earth* are you apologizing, darling?"

"Because I can't have you and have this job and have everything. And I feel like no matter what I do, Paul, I don't know what is right."

He kissed me slowly. It was clear neither of us knew what to say. It didn't matter, either. There was nothing to be done. There was no silver bullet.

"I want the same thing," Paul said. "I don't know how, but I know I have never felt like this about anyone before. I don't expect I ever will, either. You make me feel totally at ease. I want no one else."

"That's the kindest thing—"

"It is honest, Sanne. I love you. I find you irresistible. You are a comfort and my best friend. I never want you to leave. I want to wake to your face in the morning and go to bed with you at night. I want you to steal all the duvet. I won't even whinge about it."

I giggled a bit. "I do not steal them—"

"You do. I can't even fault you for it, my love. You're beautiful and perfect. Every inch of you is. I love you so much that I cannot complain."

I let out a long sigh and ran my index finger down his chest. *He* was perfect. Somehow, this person I found so upsetting in March was now beyond reproach. His foibles were now adorable. He was the most beautiful person I'd ever seen.

Paul kissed me again, pushing me on the bed.

"You know we're good together, Sanne. You know we're dynamite."

"We are."

We were interrupted by banging on the door.

"Auntie!" Marie jerked the doorknob to no avail. I was glad we locked it. "We're going to be eating dinner. What are you doing?"

"We were just talking," I answered. "We'll be right down."

"Okay. Well, you better, because I wanted to show Paul the picture I made."

"Okay, kiddo, that's fine!"

Paul chuckled and kissed me before slapping my ass. "Get moving."

"You have been waiting to do that, haven't you?" I laughed.

"I have. And I'll do it a hundred more times before I leave if you let me."

We dressed and filed to the dining room, holding hands. My sister shot me a look like she had known what we had been up to. I died to confirm it. I would do that later. She would again tell me to move to the UK. However, before I could even sit, my phone rang. It was D.C.

"This is the White House. I gotta take it." I felt important.

I was so excited as I answered in the living room. "Yes, this is Sanne Holmes-Nordgren speaking."

"Ms. Nordgren," it was Patty. "Great. I just wanted to touch base."

"Yes," I said.

"We were so glad to meet you. And we'd like to offer you the job."

My heart leapt.

Before I could say yes, she continued.

"Elaine would love for you to start in a couple of days. Would that be agreeable?"

"I'm actually out of the country at present."

I did the math. Even if I caught a flight out tomorrow, it wouldn't have worked.

"Oh," Patty sounded surprised. "She's going to be out unexpectedly, and we were hoping you could start a bit early."

I looked into the dining room. I stared at Paul as Marie talked his ear off. He smiled at me, somehow knowing they were offering me the job. He probably wished they weren't. Still, he loved me so much he was willing to be happy. It hit me right in the feels. My voice wavered.

"I uh… I have a lot of events to wrap up. I wasn't expecting it. I could start no sooner than the week after Thanksgiving, unfortunately," I said.

"Why don't you give yourself some time to think about it. We can push things a bit."

"Okay," I agreed, tears welling. "Thank you for being understanding. I will call you back tomorrow around nine?"

"Sure. Thank you. We'd be really excited to have you. Apologies for the change in schedule."

"I just have to see if I can make it work. Thanks," I said, hanging up.

"Well?" mom asked.

"Uh… they offered me the job, but I don't think I want it." I was unable to believe the words leaving my mouth.

"Why not?" Mom asked. "Is it the pay or—"

"They wanted to put me on a plane immediately."

Paul looked sad.

"I said I couldn't do that. I said I had weddings and all of that. I do. I have clients and—"

"Sweetheart, this is the opportunity of a lifetime," Mamma said. "You must. You must."

"I know," I said. "But I don't want to. I was planning on having some downtime and it doesn't *feel* right. Also, I am not sure it *is* the opportunity of a lifetime. If it doesn't feel right, it isn't."

Paul stared in disbelief. "Sanne, darling, don't do this on account of me. I can just—"

"No, Paul. I didn't do it just because of you. I know you would never ask me to decline. That's why I feel I can say no."

He shook his head, unsure where I was coming from.

"I love you, okay? You love me. You love me *a lot*. If you can find it in yourself to be happy for me, it means you would never ask me to sacrifice everything just to be right. You wouldn't make me into some stupid housewife and baby factory. You would sacrifice your own happiness—"

"But what about yours?" Paul asked. "I don't want you to settle, Sanne. You are brilliant—"

"I'm not. If I got this job, why couldn't I land another one? A job that better fits into my life? And maybe I need to take some time to figure that out. I am worthy of this job, yes, but if it makes me miss you all—everyone at this table—and affords me no time off to see you, is it really worth it? I would rather take some time off and find myself than to settle for a job that will run me into the ground. So, no, I'm not settling, baby. Not for you. Not for anyone."

Paul looked at me like I hung the moon.

"There will be the perfect job," Mom insisted. "And you're absolutely right, sweetheart. Go with your gut. Maybe it won't even be the flashiest job on Earth but it will fill your cup."

"I am privileged to be choosy, but I will be," I nodded.

Linny smiled. "I am glad you will stick around a bit."

"Me, too. I would miss you if I never got to see you again," Marie said.

"Who says you could not move to London shortly?" Mamma looked at Paul. "Right?"

"Well, visas, probably," I sighed.

"You get special status. You are Norwegian," Paul said. "Think about it. I know a place you might be able to crash—or several places. I mean, if you could put up with it being terribly humble."

I sat at the table.

"Well, I have all the choices in the world to make for another day. Tonight, though, I just want to have dinner with my favorite people on earth. Is that too much to ask?"

"Let's do it," Mom said.

Paul raised his glass. "I'd like to make a toast. To all of us finding whatever we need to be happy. And to you, Sanne, for being brave enough to go with your gut. I admire your courage and sense of self. I will try to be more like you."

"To courage and to self-awareness," I laughed.

"I can always benefit from more of that," Paul admitted.

"To growth." Linny raised her glass. "To being brave and thriving."

"To love and respect," Mom said.

"To taking the time to appreciate the people we love," Mamma added.

"To lots of tasty food!" Marie joined in.

I laughed. "Agreed!"

Everyone said a great big "cheers" except Mamma who had to chime in with "Skol" and be different.

Mamma smiled as we dug in. "Well done. We Norwegians love a toast, Paul."

"I know that," Paul winked. "I have been to enough Scandinavian weddings to know. I am no artist, but I felt compelled."

"You're plenty for me," I said. "More than enough."

Paul was not just plenty. Suddenly, he was *everything*.

That night, after dinner, we curled up under a blanket in front of the fire on the balcony. We could see a ferry crossing the fjord and not much else. The evening was still. It felt perfect somehow.

"It reminds me of Buffalo Shores," Paul said. "That place... I miss it now."

I smiled and leaned my head on his shoulder. "I do, too. Haven't been back much. Weddings are moving to the city again after the heat."

"I miss the waves. This is a balm. I see why Elisabeth likes it there. It's just so relaxed. Sometimes, a bit too much for my sense, but I even miss the person working the till always mining me for info."

I chuckled. "Daisy. Her name is Daisy and she's hardly mining. She just has a poor memory at her age. She likes you, baby."

He chuckled and linked his hand in mine under the blanket.

"It's frigid there, too, isn't it?"

"Getting that way. Summer comes in and goes before you can catch it."

Paul kissed the top of my head. "I will always miss the summer. Can we just go back in time and tell ourselves we're in love from the beginning? To spend more time?"

"I'd like that."

I would have. I would have given anything for it.

"Well, let's have many more summers—if not there, somewhere cheerful. But I'd like to get back to that little place every year. As odd as it sounds, I never felt quite so at home as there."

I smiled. "Me, either. We will. We can spend loads of time there next year."

We sat in the silence of the evening, our bodies and the thick blanket keeping us warm in front of the fire.

"Yeah. Sanne, there will be many more summers. I want you to know that. I realize you just gave up so much for me. I am serious. I want you to come to the UK."

"And crazy as it sounds, I'm up for it," I laughed. "I want that. And I didn't give it up. I decided it wasn't right for me. Something else will be. I will find it."

Paul smiled at me.

I reached out, pulling his face to mine. I leaned in and gave him a slow, deep kiss.

"We'll be okay, Paul. I know we will. And we'll go back every year and think about all of the ridiculousness we got up to."

Paul kissed me back. "Yeah. It was a mad summer. Hopefully, the start to a mad life together."

We chose one another that night and every night that followed. Whether apart or together, we were a team. There was no doubt left. Paul was mine forever. I was his for eternity. We didn't need much—not even a big wedding or a piece of paper. Life would only get sweeter, but this would never change. I may not have known it completely, but I was glad to trust it. That summer, our lives changed forever. They changed for good.

about the author

Maude Winters is a romance author who loves to write saucy fiction just like she the titles she devours. She's a horse girl through-and-through and lives in Michigan with her husband, horse girl daughter, and three dogs.

Maude loves to write strong female characters who challenge institutions and find strength in relationships with their sisters in the world.

Maude has lived throughout the world but attributes her interest in writing about the intersection of modern politics, feminism, and royalty with her time spent in the UK as a twenty-something.

loved it?

Please consider leaving a review or join my mailing list! You can find all the links <u>here</u>. Or, you can scan the QR code!

want more?

Click here or scan the code below or click here to access a free chapter of *Duke Material,* Book 3 in the Spare Change Series.

the spare change series by maude winters

From Pilot to Princess (Book 1)

Duchess Material (Book 2)

Duke Material (Book 3)
Out early 2024

Books 4 and 5 coming in 2024!

Stranded with Scrooge
Christmas Novella